P9-CFS-629

MARK RAMSDEN has played saxophone in a wide variety of professional contexts; chiefly jazz-related, although also with countless show-business luminaries, including Tom Robinson (hit single 'War Baby'). He has also been a rather speculative psychic and astrologer and has contributed to the cutting-edge sex magazine *Fetish Times*. His serious music occasionally surfaces on Radio 3 and his intimate piercings and tattoos appear far too often in various media. He is a sober alcoholic with a taste for ecstasy and sundry hallucinogenics, still clinging on to adolescence as senility beckons. He lives in London with his partner, their son and daughter, and a discarnate entity suffering from multiple personality disorder. She answers most often to the name Lola.

Also by Mark Ramsden and published by Serpent's Tail

The Dark Magus and the Sacred Whore
The Dungeonmaster's Apprentice
Radical Desire (with Housk Randall)

The
SACRED BLOOD

Mark Ramsden

Library of Congress Catalog Card Number: 2001087173

A catalogue record for this book is available from
the British Library on request

The right of Mark Ramsden to be identified as the author
of this work has been asserted by him in accordance with the
Copyright, Designs and Patents Act 1988

Copyright © 2001 Mark Ramsden

First published in 2001 by Serpent's Tail,
4 Blackstock Mews, London N4 2BT

Website: www.serpentstail.com

Phototypeset in Caslon by Intype London Ltd
Printed in Great Britain by Mackays of Chatham, plc

10 9 8 7 6 5 4 3 2 1

For Alex Jacob
Master of whips, weapons, banter and badinage

and for Dagmar
My heartbeat

1

'WAKE UP, MATT. I found more stuff about the Dungeonmaster on the net.'

'Leave me alone.'

Sasha is pouting at me from a kneeling position as she attempts to wrestle the duvet from my deathless grip. Not for the first time I can see what it would have been like to have been her father. She is so lovely – if a little tiring on a regular basis – with her flowing hennaed hair, bewitching eyes, impish smile and those dimples. It is finally possible to mention that she is thirty, just a few years after the event. (Don't tell her I told you.) But she's still a little scamp, the sort of tomboy who must have been tougher than any of the boys. She is certainly tougher than this one.

'I got mail from someone inside his organisation,' she says, 'I'm closing in on him.'

It's the American dream. Anyone can do anything.

'Look, you're in Europe now,' I tell her. 'It took thousands of years to get this depressed and useless.'

Her father was a hard man, but I bet there were times when he rued the day he created the Supreme Ogress Sasha.

There are certainly times when I wonder whether I couldn't have fallen in love with someone else. But I couldn't. She wanted it to happen, so it did. And may the Goddess have mercy upon my soul.

'Look at it this way,' she says. 'If we go after the Dungeonmaster we don't have to hide out here any more . . . '

She's timed that perfectly. It's a freezing-cold, foggy morning. And there go the church bells again. If you live anywhere sensible like a big city you may not have even noticed that someone turned the church bells off some decades ago. It's just not an issue any more. They do things differently in Bavaria. The bells in the adjacent churchyard sound every fifteen minutes. We have excellent reception, being only twenty yards away, apart from all the other churches in our little village.

It starts with four slightly out-of-tune tinny clangs for quarter-past the hour. Then, fifteen minutes later, the cracked bell chimes out an extra four. At noon and midnight it sounds out twenty-eight separate clangs, an intolerable intrusion by any standards. And why does a village this small need so many churches?

'I can't stand it,' I tell Sasha.

'It's because you are a child of Satan,' she says.

'That's good, coming from you,' I say. But my indignation only pleases her. 'And if it's not the bells it's those tractors and the birds twittering away like someone is deliberately inciting them . . . it's you. It's you, isn't it?'

Fear flickers briefly in her eyes before her smile reasserts itself. 'The bells make it more Xmassy,' she says.

To add to our problems it is fast approaching Xmas.

'I hate Xmas, and so do you,' I say.

'I used to prefer the Roman revels. Before Xianity.'

I'm not as in touch with my previous lives as Sasha is so I can't add anything to that. After some more inconclusive bickering she eventually scampers off to terrorise her pals on the Internet. By the time I stumble in for my one rationed cup of caffeinated coffee, Sasha is already doing sit-ups wearing an army vest, shorts and chunky trainers. These add an extra inch or so to her diminutive but delectable five foot two inches. She has a dagger in a sheath on her thigh, a weapon she might need to defend herself with if I have to listen to any more of this stuff.

' . . . we can charge people to look at our latest work. We don't need a gallery any more. We can exhibit on the Net. It's the same with my films. I can still get my work out there.'

And about the same amount of people would look at it. Because she is not famous and therefore – in her eyes – worthless.

'Sasha, we are never going to be celebrities. In fact, we can't be famous any more. Unless you want us to kill a few more people. Then you could be the female Manson. The evil genius who manipulates others into killing . . .'

Her eyes narrow, she gasps and then she draws her cute little dagger and hurls it at me. It misses by a few feet, embedding itself exactly in a picture of my face – not the present collapsed useless one but the smaller, firmer one I used to have. 'Yes!' says Sasha, raising her arms in triumph. It's comforting to know that she wasn't trying to kill me – for once – but the blade has ripped the photo apart. We are left with a conceptual work symbolising the effect she had on me when we met – and the effect she still has. But an important visual resource has now been lost for ever.

There is no longer any proof that I once had blond hair, or even hair at all. There is no proof that I could once be persuaded to smile for the camera – if the lovely Sasha asked me nicely. The dagger has obliterated the last surviving evidence of Matt Jackson, the person I used to be. And it's a shame. I quite liked that guy. I don't like the new name on my false passport, and I don't like the grumpy old git I have become. I'm just past forty in earth years but something is broken inside. Although I can still rant and rave. I'm good at that.

'You could have killed me!' I tell her.

'I don't kill people Matt. You do. Remember?'

Now she puts it that way I suppose she has a point. Except that she killed her first husband. He may well have been sick, in mind and body, but society usually prefers euthanasia to be practised on people about fifty years older, if at all.

'Spider Bates,' I say, mentioning the clod in question. He was a rock star, one of two Sasha has helped to the other side, although she is technically innocent in both cases.

'You are *so* in denial,' she says. 'It's you who keeps on killing people.'

I take the knife out of my picture. It's a bit unnerving having your face split in two and quite possibly a bad omen, not that we are superstitious or anything.

'Did you really mean the dagger to land there?' I ask.

'I have been practising. It's part of the Ninefold Initiation. The Warrior Arts.'

My heart sinks. I'm supposed to be doing the same training. So we can infiltrate the Black Order, a group of Satanic Nazis, some of whom tried to kill us last year. The Order are pretty damned serious about having well-trained motivated troops. My current schedule includes learning old Norwegian, three different runic alphabets and medieval German. I should also be running up and down hills with a full backpack and taking long swims in ice-cold rivers. And that's just the start. The complete Nazi – sorry, Odinist – should be adept at runecraft, sword- and stick-fighting, speech-making, honour and nobility, brewing beer and, for all I know, removing their hats when a lady enters the room. So far, I have managed a little research into 'seething' – a Viking rage-based sorcery that seems strangely familiar. Its sex magic aspects were thought to be 'unmanly' and were suppressed by the Xians, which was a shame. If they had left in the sodomy and the cross-dressing the Xian Church could have counted on my support.

'I hope you're keeping up,' says Sasha. 'They'll know if you haven't trained.'

'I'm hoping to get by as a sort of John Steed figure. You know, bumble about with a pleasant smile and occasionally flourish an umbrella or something. You can do all the fighting if you like.'

'He was a *gentleman*,' she says. Which is great coming from a bloody colonial. 'And, anyway, if you don't do the basic training we won't get past novice grade.'

And then we would stand far less chance of being horribly massacred a long way from home, which would never do. Although we have no 'home' anyway. There are ongoing murder investigations in England and America which may involve us one of these days. The charges are valid. A guilty verdict might ensue, if you're going to be all judgemental about it. But they started it. They did. It's never us. It's always them.

'Someone has to expose these people,' says Sasha. I say something vaguely Buddhist to the tune of: it's best not to meddle. Leave things alone. They're supposed to be like that. She just pumps iron through that bit, as if my speech was a light drizzle that pleasantly enhanced her exercise routine.

'Sasha! I don't have the time to waste on this. I'm older, eleven years closer to being dead than you are. Get some investigative journalist to do it. We could go and live somewhere warm. You could spend the rest of your life being worshipped by good-looking young men.'

'I don't want "young men". I want you.'

Her eyes are big and gooey. She loves me. She wants me.

And if that isn't proof that she is clinically insane I don't know what is.

2

DURING THE SECOND hour of Sasha's pep talk I pick her beret up and throw it Frisbee-style. It lands exactly on her head, triggering a broad smile. 'Beret!' I say, stressing the second syllable. She takes the hat off and lofts it back. But she aims too high.

'Over my head,' I tell her, as I go to retrieve it.

'Like my art,' she says. Fighting talk. Perhaps she is annoyed because she failed to complete a 'beret'. It's my turn again. Whenever anyone tells you it's a good idea to move to the countryside, just remember that you will probably end up doing things like this.

My next attempt scores a full 'beret', despite Sasha's infringement of the no-pouting rule. We both like this game. Every time I land the hat exactly on her head I am rewarded with a smile from the most beautiful woman in the world, and every time she lands the beret on my head, not quite as often I have to say, she is rewarded by the sight of me looking like a complete and utter burk, something she apparently never tires of.

'Stefan's invited us round!' says Sasha, deliberately bouncing up and down on the couch so that the level of decaff in my mug comes dangerously close to slopping over the side. It's provocative behaviour. Designed to make me take immediate action. But I'm still in a sulk about her obsession with the Dungeonmaster. As if killing another father figure is likely to change anything. She's still going to be Sasha Kristinson, her father's daughter. And there's no cure to being your parents' child. Except having some children yourself and fucking up so badly that you eventually have to forgive your own parents. But that's time-consuming. So they tell me.

' . . . Stefan could lead us to the Dungeonmaster . . . '

Not that again. We met our landlord Stefan through a small ad in a Nazi newspaper. Such things are legally on sale at any newsagent in Germany. I used to find this upsetting until I read one and found that the editorial stance was hardly any different from many British mainstream papers, never mind the one that uses a Gothic typeface. The *National Zeitung* doesn't like asylum-seekers, single mothers and working women in general. It fetishises meat-eating, military history and anything else that started about five hundred years ago and has never changed since. The countryside is the soul of the nation. We would all be a lot better off if we lived like we did during the war when the whole country pulled together. The European Union is the work of Satan. They really should print an edition for the English heartlands. They'd clean up.

The reason we were reading such a newspaper in the first place is that Sasha thought it was a way into the Black Order. She just has to solve a riddle set by someone who crucified a cat on our front door. Who is the Dungeonmaster's Apprentice? And who is the Dungeonmaster himself? Is he a leader of a sinister occult sect which is directing one of the many local neo-Nazi movements? Can he be the force behind the dread Nazi music industry which seeks to enslave our youth with Black Metal and skinhead rock music? I used to think this idea was ridiculous until I found out how many CDs they sell. They can't get mainstream media coverage, but their stuff hooks a lot of thrill-seekers on the Internet. With most of Russia destabilised and the rest of Europe struggling to cope with loss of national identity, they could well be a force to be reckoned with in the near future. Sasha is always banging on about this. Until I start agreeing with her. Then she is legally obliged to say the exact opposite of what I have just said.

'It *is* quite frightening,' I tell her.

'I don't know,' she says. 'Most kids want to party.'

Which is true. And easy to forget while living in this freezing grey fog. The youth still prefer dancing in Ibiza to having their bollocks shot off in Stalingrad. And long may they continue to do so. Mind you, cut off their supply of soap operas and Ecstasy and there's no telling what might happen.

' . . . you just sit there pontificating all day,' she says. 'Why should men just tell the rest of the world what to do?'

I must have missed something. How did we get there again?

'I hadn't noticed men *did* rule the world. I don't anyway. Anyway, more women than men voted for Hitler. Did you know that?'

It's all gone quiet over there.

'And what if we do unmask the Dungeonmaster? The citizens find out he's in favour of hard work, the family and keeping the Gypsies out. They'll probably make him World President. For ever. That's what people are like.'

'You're so negative.'

'Maybe it's the cold, dear. You know, it would actually be warmer in jail. Much warmer.'

'Some homicidal maniac would make you his wife.'

'She already did. Remember?'

Sasha blows me a kiss. You would never know from her reaction that I am quite angry now. She says I have King Canute syndrome – trying to stop the tide coming in. She goes as far as calling it the male condition. Fruitless rage against the encroaching female waves. That's as may be. We men can still storm out of the house in a huff, which I'm going to do any minute now.

Sasha's back on the laptop, clicking and clattering at the keys. 'What? Oh no! Tracey Morgan has won an award for best sex worker of the year!' she says.

'You didn't even enter,' I say, very quietly and calmly. 'You don't even live in England any more. You are legally dead . . . '

'It's not about *me*,' she says, without stopping to think if she should ever say such a thing. 'Tracey is just so lucky. Someone gave her a flat. In Knightsbridge!'

There is a pause while we both try to ignore the fact that I haven't given her an immensely valuable piece of real estate. Nor am I likely to. We are presently residing in a two-room shack attached to a farm in darkest Bavaria. Yuletide is approaching, which means the days are short and the nights are long. It is extremely cold. We have one cold tap, an outside toilet and an oil oven which may be poisoning us. The way to enjoy such conditions is to go native. We should eat large amounts of roast meat and drink copious amounts of gluhwein. Ingolstadt, the nearest town, has cute little huts where the natives gather to shine up their chunky faces with hot sweet booze. But we are alcoholic drug addicts. Clean and sober. Just for today. While eating tofu and herbal tea.

Lucky old us. And there go the bells again. When I have finished ritually cursing every single bellringer who has ever lived, I notice that Sasha has drawn an amusing caricature of myself and propped it up on our mantelpiece.

Some men might take offence at a portrait of themselves with a Hitler moustache addressing what appears to be a Nuremberg rally in our kitchen. I'm just glad she's speaking to me, albeit through the medium of her art. It's nice to see her resorting to pencil on paper also, instead of a shaky three-hour video about nothing, starring nobody and intentionally signifying nothing. Sasha's art is not for narrative junkies like myself, or people who cling pathetically to the idea that an artist might actually be 'good' at something. Unfortunately for her, you can't sell that junk without being famous. Which she can never be without being arrested.

'Do you like it, Matt? It's a drawing. *Something I actually did myself.*'

The venom in her last statement comes from the valid charge that many 'artists' just nick everything and then claim irony as a defence. But how hard is it to draw a circle for my bald head, some scars and a Hitler moustache? I could have done that. I might *even* have managed the idea myself. But I would never think up what Sasha says next.

'It's time we got married again,' she says. 'We could get two new identities and have another wedding.'

'You're such a romantic,' I say wearily. And if you think getting married once is a drag, just imagine if you had to keep on doing it every time you change identity. I am now a connoisseur of municipal registry offices, musty churches, pebbly beaches, windswept hills.

'Go on! We never got married at Xmas.'

'What does Stefan want? We paid him upfront for three months.'

'I think he would do very well as one of my knights. One of my loyal servants who will destroy the evil king.'

'He's a card-carrying Nazi! Why would he help you find the Dungeonmaster?'

'He will lead us to him. *Because* his parents are real Nazis. And, anyway, he's in love with me.'

For a few seconds she's smiling and I'm frowning. And then we return to our original tasks. I have some grumbling to do and Sasha has a world to save.

3

Stefan's welcoming smile could melt a polar icecap. As he's gorgeous it's hard not to return it. He has twinkling blue eyes and wavy blond hair which flops down over cheekbones most women would kill for. He is hyper-fit, happy and rich; and I don't even mind, which gives you some idea of how seductive that smile is. He leads us through to an alpine-kitsch sitting room full of grim family portraits stretching back to the dawn of photography. Stefan's parents are visiting relatives in Texas, so he is presently alone, preening himself in this Bavarian ranch-house. A grandfather clock starts to chime the hour just before the village churches crank into action. The resultant clash of tinkling chimes and booming bells is exquisitely discordant. As is Sasha's attempt to converse in her rusty German.

Stefan politely struggles on with her for a while but his American English is too good for us to carry on suffering. We will have to do better than this, though, if we are going to be accepted by the Dungeonmaster. We can both speak German – it's in our blood – but Bavarian is proving a harder nut to crack. The local dialect has the same relationship to

German as medieval Scottish has to English. The endings of most words are slurred into something else. It wouldn't be so bad in nearby Munich, but Sasha wanted to visit her father's birthplace, so here we are. The impenetrable local dialect reminds me of all those silly spy novels where someone gets off a plane and manages to pass for a native speaker of the language. Never mind about regional accents, dialects, idioms and the local culture – the stuff you have to live somewhere for thirty years to know about. Try faking that.

'You should have told me it was fancy dress,' says Sasha to our host.

It's cheeky, but she does have a point. Stefan is wearing: one shiny pair of black brogues made by some old chap in Mayfair; a pair of thick grey woollen knee-socks with a green garter tucked into the fold; one kilt and waistcoat made out of dingy green scratchy wool with white windowpanes in; one dismal old check shirt with regimental tie tied in very small knot. His shirt collar shows signs of wear in the traditional English upper-class manner which I believe is meant to demonstrate that one could afford to buy a new shirt but one is deliberately not going to. He has accessorised this ensemble with a silver watch chain, a black tasselled sporran and a grey felt triby – a considerable improvement on the pith helmet he once arrived in. On that occasion Sasha had to dash out to the bathroom, from where she could be clearly heard suppressing shrieks of laughter. He is not wearing a monocle or spats or a cummerbund, but he actually does possess these items – being rather fond of dressing up. He sometimes looks like a German undercover agent posted into England during the Second World War, one of those poor sods they told to read P.G. Wodehouse in order to find out how best to blend in with the natives. He has many traditional German costumes of course: militaria dating back a thousand years to the Knights Templar – so he says. He may well be a buffoon, but his father is rich enough to be able to summon up packs of rabid Nazi skinheads to do his bidding. He has several big houses to scuttle back to while the useful idiots go to jail. Or to hospital to have their bones set.

So our landlord is a camp Anglophile Bavarian Nazi who occasionally wears a pith helmet – in tribute to our long-lost empire-builders. Matt's lost it again, you are saying. That just couldn't happen. But you must be familiar with the sight of Japanese families buying Burberry raincoats in London. Some of the French Bon-Chic-Bon-Genre apparently try to look like posh English country folk. I once saw top American crime novelist James Ellroy kitted out in a kilt which he must have thought was . . . well, I can't imagine what he thought he was doing. I used to be an English jazz musician and what could be more inappropriate than that? At least in the eyes, especially the *eyes* of the public, bless them. The point is it's hard to appropriate someone else's culture without looking a little bit silly. That includes white Radio One DJs who glorify the gangsta lifestyle (and get shot in the process. Oh how we laughed . . .) and our Bavarian landlord who has decided to adopt what he thinks are the dress and manners of an English country gentleman. I am using Nazi in the original sense of the word here, and not to mean 'an assertive person with whom I disagree' or 'any resident of Germany past or present' with which it is often confused.

The centrepiece of Stefan's excessively neat and tidy coffee table is an antique cigarette lighter. Stefan spends far too long trying to make it work. I would have smashed it to bits by now, but he is clearly a little less ill.

'Have you fire?' he says, with a rueful glance at his malfunctioning lighter. He means: have you got a light?

'I don't smoke.'

'Like the Führer himself,' he says, smiling triumphantly.

I smile to share his joke, for that was how his remark was intended. Even as my ribs are still aching from the aftermath of this, I remember that Hitler's fanatical anti-smoking campaign was even less successful than his thousand-year Reich. They certainly like their tobacco in Germany. There are cigarette machines on every street corner, thick clouds of smoke in every bar. It makes you wonder why they don't all drop dead quicker than we do. It must be all that marching around in the fresh air. Now I'm indulging in cheap anti-German rhetoric, like all the little Englanders do (including the liberals). While calling themselves anti-racists.

Soon his cigarette is lit and the smoke is drifting inexorably into my lungs.

'You must drink then!' he says. 'I have some fine Bavarian beer.'

He shows me a bottle with a fat laughing friar on it. It's the best beer in the world, but I can't drink it. I shake my head glumly. 'No thank you.'

'I have German wine.'

Not so good but it still works. And I still can't drink it. 'No thank you.'

'Sekt?'

That's the German equivalent of champagne. Which I can't drink. 'No thank you. Mineral water will be fine.'

'I have some very special single-malt Scotch whisky. Lagavulin,' he says.

'No thanks!' I say, so loudly that he actually takes a step backwards with a puzzled look on his face. For some reason a large proportion of the population seem to think that alcoholism doesn't actually exist and what we need is 'just one drink'. To cheer us up. But we don't mind. Not really. It only happens every time we go out of the house. I catch sight of my face in the mirror and realise that what I thought was a normal expression is in fact more appropriate to the start of a knockdown, drag-out fight. Sasha is making that face which means: 'Apologise! You dolt!'

'Sorry, Stefan. I didn't sleep. Can I have a mineral water?'

'Me too, please!' says Sasha. The landlord looks like he is about to burst into tears. Two mineral waters! What will the neighbours say?

One of Sasha's loveliest smiles sorts that one out, then Stefan scurries off and returns with our mineral waters, handing them to us as if they were explosive devices that might go off at any minute. Now we all have a drink it's time for the toast, an event of great ritual significance in Bavaria.

Stefan raises his glass. 'So! Prosit!' he says, rather muffled and subdued.

With our two mineral waters outnumbering his one real drink you might as well toast the successful planning application for a local asylum-seekers' home.

'Perhaps there is one local tradition you can join me in,' he says, brightening as he raises his glass to a kitsch oil-painting of Der Führer. We do so and then we can sit down and admire the landlord's collection of Hitler kitsch: knives, guns, badges, uniforms and photos. It may be real for all I know. It is certainly expensive.

'This is a fascinating collection,' says Sasha. Her eyes are sparkling, the little liar. 'You must have worked very hard to find all these things.'

Few men could resist having their pride and joy praised by Sasha. Stefan certainly can't. He is smiling broadly. He doesn't even mind us drinking mineral water any more. After he has taken us through his collection it's time for Sasha to mention the Black Order.

'The Black Order,' says Stefan, smiling roguishly. 'Which one? There are many pretenders to the Crown.'

'There is only one Dungeonmaster. And he is surely the leader of the only sect which is worthy of the name.'

'And how would a charming young lady such as you know this? Magickal secrets are only passed on from mouth to ear. You can only have read about this.'

'I knew Richard Ambrose. Alice Hathaway-Turner.'

Stefan has stopped smiling.

'If you knew anything about the Black Order you would know they were interlopers. Thrill-seekers. The real work has taken thousands of years to come to fruition.'

Sasha is now using a rare interrogation technique of hers known as shutting-the-fuck-up-for-a-change. It can be devastating. But Stefan doesn't fall for it. Eventually she has to beg. 'Look, we want to help him. We are ready to serve. It's in my blood. My grandfather was a member of the Brotherhood of Saturn.'

The Brotherhood of Saturn was a German sex magic sect infiltrated and eventually wrecked by Aleister Crowley. I never knew Sasha's grandfather was involved. It seems rather unlikely, come to think of it. If Sasha wasn't a woman of the highest possible integrity and probity I might almost think she is lying.

'He was German?' asks Stefan.

'He lived in Munich, where my father was born. My dad

was one of those brave young boys who were conscripted at the end of the war.'

Now that's actually true. But I can't picture her grim ogre of a father as an apple-cheeked child. Although somewhere underneath very many layers of ice I can even feel something for Sasha's dad. How could anyone ever recover from *that*? I must be getting soft.

'I thought you were German,' says Stefan, to me. There's always someone who thinks a bald head and a leather jacket are proof positive of German blood but I just shake my head. While silently grinding my teeth.

Sasha picks up one of the knives and holds it reverently aloft. The handle is inlaid with black and red swastikas. From the moment I see this item I need to own it. I have no idea why. I am supposedly above the urge to accumulate things, but something inside me is screaming that I must possess this item. And many more like it. Because it's bad. The *baddest* thing ever. And a lot of people feel the same way. Nazi kitsch is big business. Just as with cocaine, you don't even need the genuine product. Any old rubbish will do, and people pay top dollars anyway. You are selling the eternal glamour of evil, a chance to dance with the devil. The punters just can't stop themselves. Sasha certainly can't leave the knife alone, turning it to watch the play of light on the blade.

'It's not for sale, I'm afraid,' says Stefan, as he watches Sasha stroking and cuddling her new toy.

She pouts briefly and then starts in on Stefan again, her voice colder and harder now she has been defied by a mere man. 'I'm interested in Hitler's initiation into the secret societies of Munich just after the First World War.'

Stefan's eyes glitter, but it's difficult to know whether it's because he fancies her or because he knows about this stuff.

'There are many books telling the story of the right-wing esotericists who guided Hitler. And these theories are now being spread by Black Metal musicians.'

'That Satanic stuff?' says Sasha. 'Isn't that just for spotty teenagers?'

'Spotty teenagers who grow into strong men. In any case, Satanism is an important step on the way to the real rebellion – nationalism. And the real enemy will always be the Jewish-derived fiction of Xianity. Little boys can hardly shock their mummies by holding a black mass these days. There are less and less Xians left to outrage.'

Although no shortage of church bells. Which have just gone off again. It's almost enough to make you want to join Stefan's side for real. But even Hitler couldn't wean the masses off Catholicism, eventually coming to a series of messy compromises with the Pope and his local franchise-sellers.

'We must somehow oppose the consumer culture of America,' says Stefan. 'Moronic movies! Terrible food! We must fight for our identity! Or we will drown in hamburgers and Coca-Cola!'

I couldn't agree more. Which is a bit worrying really. He's not the sort of man I want to be agreeing with.

'The Black Metal kids are fighting for European culture,' says Stefan, and I can't disagree with that either. There must be some way I can distance myself from Stefan and his mates.

'Those guys take themselves far too seriously,' I say.

'Humour is for the weak,' says Stefan. 'The strong have no need of it.'

Which is a shame. I like a laugh myself.

'Isn't one of them doing twenty years for murder?' asks Sasha.

'Yeah,' I say, reluctant to mention his real name as he will be out in about another fifteen years. 'At least he burned some churches down before he started killing anyone who wasn't a "real man". He's one of my favourite comedians, actually. Who could resist his plaintive cry that the first jails he was incarcerated in were not sufficiently uncomfortable for him? Apparently Odin would never have stood for being imprisoned anywhere you could have your own stereo. And then there's his views on people with brown eyes.'

'Brown eyes?' queries Sasha.

'He says it's like looking at their arseholes. People with brown eyes are especially keen racists because they are afraid of being black. They know that they are not as Ayran as people with blue eyes.'

'And people take this guy seriously?'

'More and more of them. Of course, being in jail helps. Every messiah figure should be imprisoned at some point. Jesus, Hitler, Manson.'

Sasha is nodding slowly, perhaps seeing herself working through an unjust incarceration, keeping in touch with her troops, writing her prison diaries. Well, it might be stimulating to picture her in one of those bad-girls-behind-bars videos she used to make me watch. The one consolation of being involved in this suicidal quest to find the Dungeon-master is that she no longer has time for trash culture. Nothing will divert her from her true path – getting us all killed before she develops any more wrinkles. (Which look perfectly lovely, dear. Oh never mind.)

Stefan excuses himself, saying he needs to make an important phone call. When we are sure he is out of earshot Sasha starts a vitriolic critique of the soft furnishings.

'It's his father's place,' I tell her. 'Just be thankful we are not making small talk with some sixty-year-old farmer.'

'You could probably bond with him easily enough. The older you get.'

'You will be your father's daughter one day,' I say, a particularly low blow.

Papa certainly remains a ghost at the feast. There are occasions when some of Sasha's facial expressions are reminiscent of the old warrior. These occasions are becoming more frequent as the years pass. And what is she up to now? Getting a small army together in order to declare war. Where *does* she get it from?

'You'll end up like him. And . . . ' I have to shut up because Sasha is about to cry. For the first few years of our relationship this was a signal for instant cease-fire. I used to think Sasha could get off a plane in Belfast, burst into tears and even the Irish would stop squabbling.

'If you think I'm going to breed nine children and make them all apple strudel . . . '

'You're Catholic. It can never really be eradicated. It's waiting for you. Somewhere in your future.' And somewhere in mine, perhaps. Dreaming of the bad old days while virtuous little Sasha puts a sensible hat on to go to Mass.

'At least we know Stefan's not kinky,' I tell her. 'You were definitely wrong about that.'

Sasha does a little seethe but recovers quickly. She isn't going to waste energy on arguing with me when she could be taking little digital pictures with her hand-held computer. She may have been taping Stefan too. This is her evidence. What she will present to the world when we have found and defeated the Dungeonmaster. After which she will be carried aloft through the streets by cheering crowds.

Stefan returns, having slipped into something a little less comfortable.

He is naked apart from a pony's bridle. He has a tooled leather crop in his teeth. From the eager acquiescent look on his face we could use this to redden his taut little bum or perhaps even give him a sound Mapplethorping – the insertion of a crop handle where the sun don't shine – as performed by Mr Mapplethorpe in a famous self-portrait.

Stefan has rubbed some horsy linament on his body to make his taut thigh muscles gleam. His tackle is stuck through a gleaming iron ring and getting more tumescent as we circle him, appraising him from various angles.

'You got a tail?' Sasha asks.

He nods towards a leather saddlebag, inside which are various equine accoutrements. It's cute watching Sasha saddle him up.

'No hooves?' she says.

He shakes his head shamefacedly. I don't know: amateurs. Sasha smiles over at me. She doesn't have to remind me that she was completely right and I was . . . not in full possession of the facts at the time I made my preliminary assessment.

'Forgive me,' says Stefan, 'but I heard you whipping each other the other night. I thought you would like to see some of my other outfits. I, too, am a pervert.'

Well, that's not a word we like to use, but as he's rather beautiful neither Sasha nor I say anything.

'You take me to the fetish clubs of London,' says Stefan. 'And I get you a meeting with a representative of the Dungeonmaster. This is a fair exchange.'

Sasha walks over to me and hooks her arm around my waist. I hear her give a soft sigh of satisfaction as she fixes Stefan with an imperious glance.

His head bows immediately. She points at the floor between her feet, at which he scampers over and starts to reverently kiss her pointy little boots.

4

In the Satanic Tarot the Hermit is represented by Hitler portrayed as a penniless artist in pre-First World War Vienna. From the pocket of his tattered coat protrudes a score of Wagner's Ring and a guide to Norse mythology.

The Complete Guide to the Tarot

I WAKE UP clutching part of a ponyboy's tail. There is straw in our bed and a faint lingering smell of leather and amyl nitrate. The recollection of a number of startling events is swift – and extremely pleasurable. Surely this new playmate will keep Sasha too busy to drag me off to some frozen Nazi castle? But I can't quiz her on this because she is elsewhere, perhaps rubbing some healing salve on Stefan's well-whipped flanks. I go in search of my little equestrian beauty, only to find that she is scrabbling away at the laptop keys, her eyes glowing in the radioactive light of our screen.

'I found an information resource on the Dungeonmaster!' she tells me. 'There's a chatroom for German pagans! It seems that . . .'

Stefan's Nazi dagger is within easy reach. It's sharp enough to kill the two of us. If I was to pick it up and use it I would undoubtedly save the lives of all those who will perish as a result of whatever folly Sasha is presently planning. A beneficial side-effect would be that I am no longer able to process incoming information. Stuff like this: ' . . . some believe he is capable of human sacrifice . . . ' Yeah, yeah. I find our wooden coffee grinder and settle down to grinding high-roast decaff beans while Sasha grinds on at me about the Dungeonmaster. Now I like a good gossip, being a bit of a girl myself, but unfortunately Sasha isn't going to stop at malicious and enjoyable speculation about other people's private lives. She has a plan. The Dungeonmaster must be stopped at all costs. ' . . . a number of unexplained disappearances . . . '

Grinding the beans doesn't put her off, and neither does washing out the cafetière or boiling the water in a silly little pot with an electric filament stuck in it. No one has heard of kettles in Bavaria. While I scald my hand pouring thee water into the cafetière, I recall Bertie Wooster refusing to listen to something Bingo Little was trying to tell him, on the grounds that he hadn't yet had his morning tea. His plaintive pre-tea bleating didn't wash with Bingo, and I'm not even going to try with Sasha.

' . . . using the money from the Death Metal CDs and merchandise to support Croatian militia. His father was a famous pilot, decorated by *Hitler himself* . . . '

Her face lights up, as it often does when somebody or something is deemed to be famous. Especially if Sasha has some connection – however peripheral – with fame, however fleeting or undeserved. The connection here is that she has discovered this information. So it's hers. It doesn't belong to whoever found it out or made it up.

' . . . thirty-seven accredited kills. That must have been like being a Nazi pop star . . . '

I look at the trees outside our window. ' . . . bare ruined choirs, where late the sweet birds sang . . . ' As far as I know it's mandatory to do that quote whenever denuded trees appear. Anyway, there they are, somehow resolute against everything the cold, cruel German winter can throw at them. They have lost their leaves, I have lost my hair and Sasha has lost her mind.

' . . . it's thought that the Dungeonmaster never recovered from his harsh distant father or his clinging mother. She made him insufferably egotistic while encouraging him to live up to his father's memory . . . '

The mirror is telling me that my once-magnificent chest is fast becoming a memory. I'm too depressed to exercise. Even though I know it's the only cure for depression. I'm almost as flat as Sasha. 'Bare ruined tits where late my sweet pectorals sang.'

' . . . the old Viking custom of sacrificing nine species every winter. Something to represent each species. And some human beings.'

'I like the order you put that in,' I tell her. 'So he's going to murder a human being. And some dumb animals. In a ritual sacrifice. And he's announced this in advance on the Internet, has he?'

'I got it from an occult webzine opposed to him.'

'Well, if it's in black and white it must be true.'

'They had someone on the inside. Someone who went missing. Maybe even killed. The Dungeonmaster is a killer. He's a killer!'

So are you, dear. But do go on.

' . . . and we could stop him!' She is following me around

now, looking for approval from her grumpy daddy. Why am I annoyed? She has tried so hard to please me. At least that is what she genuinely believes right now. The onlooker may think that she has merely been doing what I do occasionally – loading up on any old junk on the Internet – rather than think about the junk inside me.

She's still at it. ' . . . according to the Pagan Zone he has a genuine Picasso! And a Matisse!'

My coffee won't be cold enough to drink for a while, but at least I can snuff up its aromatic steam. Delightful. And to think I spent my formative years drinking stewed tea made from floor sweepings.

'We don't know anyone here,' continues Sasha. 'We must travel to England and mobilise an army to move against him. We need to infiltrate the Animal Liberation Front. They really hate anyone who kills animals just for the fun of it.'

'Yes. They're also not keen on people infiltrating them. I mean they're fanatics, aren't they?'

'So am I,' says Sasha with a winning smile. This contains the right amount of dimples, bright shining eyes, pearly white teeth and a little air kiss to finish off with. But she's still going to get us both killed.

'We need some people who are passionate about animals and the scum who mistreat them,' says Sasha. 'We need some guy with lots of money . . . '

'One of your slaves,' I supply.

'One of the paying ones,' she says, smiling at me.

'Oh yeah? And what was that you were doing last night? When we finally packed Stefan off to bed?'

'Enslaving *you*,' she says. And only the angriest college girl would want to disagree. First we started with a long tussle because both of us wanted to be receivers rather than givers

– or submissive, as some might say. Then she won, as she invariably does, whatever game we are playing. So I had to do all the work – or 'dominate' her, as some still say. Although keeping up with Sasha is certainly slavery by any definition of the word.

We seem to have drifted off her plans for getting us all killed, but these eight-hour sex and transcendence sessions tend to linger in the memory. Of course, many people prefer football. Or home improvements. I do apologise.

'. . . we need a rich guy, someone with weapons. And a small army of dedicated men and women who don't mind using them.'

'What type of weapons?' I ask.

'Guns,' she says, matter of fact. 'He's armed. So we have to be.'

'No one else cares enough about animal rights,' I say. That stops Sasha in her tracks for the moment.

'*You* might not. But a lot of people *do*. And we can take the Dungeonmaster's money. And treasure. Paintings. Jewellery. Valuable manuscripts.'

Suddenly I flash back to one of my previous lives as one of Hitler's generals. Having to sit there and humour der Führer while he comes up with really great ideas. Like having a battle at a place called Stalingrad. Great idea. Let's start in winter.

'How on earth would you know that?' I ask.

'Stefan told me.'

'Why would he tell you?'

'He's crazy about me. He told me while you took a leak. He knows it's hopeless, but he just wanted to tell me. Don't look so grumpy! Men *like* me.'

I know that. Why she thinks it needs proving so often is

beyond me. She once had a shrink who told her it was poor self-esteem that made her want to shag everyone she ever meets. If only I could get to see more of this 'poor self-esteem'.

'We need some tough guys who hate Nazis, or vivisectionists,' says Sasha, as if I could do anything to facilitate this. 'Or maybe just some bad guys who know how to sell the paintings. It would be nice never to have to work again.'

'It's debatable whether most people would consider that occasionally whipping rich guys is actually work. You know – poorly paid drudgery. Like everyone else does.'

'We would have to go back to London. To find our tough guys.'

Now she has me hooked. A trip to London. A trip anywhere away from these bloody bells. And there they go again as another quarter hour has passed, clang clang clang clang. Clang clang clang clang. Then another ten seconds in which the bells linger on, soaking themselves deep into my bones, taunting me, mocking my feeble attempts to put authoritarian Xianity behind me. And once we are back in London, a bell-free zone, we may never have to return.

'It's a good idea,' I tell her. 'It's like King Arthur travelling the length and breadth of the land, trying to find the bravest knights to search for the Holy Grail.'

Her frown is telling me there is something wrong with that comparison.

'Or Queen Sasha,' I add. 'Who will be brave enough to serve her? Who will lay down their life for the fairest maiden of them all?'

She nuzzles up for a few kisses and a group hug. I know there's only two of us, but Sasha believes we are both victims of multiple-personality syndrome – even though this is no longer fashionable and therefore can't possibly be true. She might be right, though. There's a lot of us in this couple. A host of demons, as the Xians might say.

But I don't have to travel to London to find the Holy Grail. My grail is my favourite coffee cup, from which I can drink in perfect peace and quiet untroubled by the need to mobilise a team of fearless assassins. This cup is even designed to remind astrology enthusiasts that Cancerians are home-lovers. Upon it a cute, cuddly crab is depicted close to a glinting silver moon. A list of luminescent Cancerian qualities is headed by the word 'Home-loving'. Whether such a cautious crab should have hitched itself to a fiery ram like Sasha is highly debatable. I hold the cup up to the grey morning light.

'I never noticed the red heart on this thing before,' I tell her.

'They should have made it a black heart,' she says. 'Like yours.'

She can talk. The Black Widow.

'Where are you going to recruit these troops of yours? On the Internet?'

'We meet them face to face.' All of a sudden her face splits open into a delightful smile and it is clear that we might be able to indulge in a certain amount of debauchery.

'We can go to a few parties. I had a look on the BDSM channel.'

This is where the bondage and s/m community swap scurrilous gossip and play status games. I prefer Seinfeld myself. But if the Internet hadn't been invented there would be no way Sasha could even know all this. She wouldn't be obsessed by what some silly little boys do in the name of Black Metal, Satan or their supposed 'Aryan' heritage. She could get herself a nice Jane Austen book out of the library. And I could get some tropical fish. They're very soothing, apparently.

'I found explicit instructions for animal sacrifice. And ritual sex with horses. He must be stopped!'

'It's a wind-up. They probably don't do it.'

She shows me the photographs. The text.

'It's a fake,' I say, faking it myself. The Dungeonmaster's horse resources may or may not be a fake. But someone somewhere has been handing out a lot of sugar cubes.

'This can't be right,' I tell her, hoping she will swallow this blatant lie. 'Any serious Nazi has to be careful about his image these days. Now they can actually get elected.'

'Maybe he doesn't want political power,' she says. 'He's rich. He has a private army. What does he care about going on the telly and pretending to be normal?'

'Maybe.'

'Even if it is a fake,' she tells me, 'they still inspire people. Someone has to teach him a lesson. Come on! You know they kill defenceless animals. It is one of the paths to power.'

'So why aren't Ronald McDonald or Colonel Sanders the greatest black magicians of all time?' Sasha's eyes close as she takes a deep breath. Soon I am being pinned to the wall by the force of her animal rights rhetoric. I keep on agreeing with her, like an innocent woman forced by the Inquisition to admit that she is a witch. But it doesn't stop the torture.

'. . . the Dungeonmaster must be stopped! Just imagine if the Germans had actually killed Hitler in one of their assassination attempts. How many lives might have been saved?'

She is smiling at me hopefully. But the only picture in my head is what happened to the conspirators – a show trial then slow strangulation by piano wire. I really must channel her energies somewhere where fewer people might get killed. Art, for instance. Or the sort of lewd show business that used to pay our rent. It's high time we went back to organising sex parties, a profitable and absorbing hobby. Where you don't get killed.

' . . . and now we have the Internet we can mobilise our forces against these men! We can certainly destroy a few rich so-called Satanists!'

Who is this 'we', I want to ask but there is no space to do so. I am being swept along in the tide of Sasha's rhetoric.

' . . . he might have a metal detector to deal with his mail, but that doesn't mean that a motivated individual can't dynamite his castle . . . ' After a few more minutes of this the trees outside are starting to shake. Some might put this down to the storm that has been brewing all week, but I know better. It is Sasha who is causing the earth to tremble. ' . . . and when you infiltrate his inner circle . . . '

'What? What happened to "us"? Why am "I" doing this?'

'They will never let a woman anywhere near the source of power.'

'What about his stuff on the Net? That seems to feature female flesh altars, the consumption of the wise blood. Orthodox Satanism seems quite keen on women.'

'As something for the high priest to shag,' she says. 'When was the last time you saw a woman at the head of one of these evil empires?'

Without having to think about it too long I can picture Margaret Thatcher, the Queen of England and my mum. And a certain pint-sized American who seems to be strutting around in metaphorical jackboots yet again. Maybe it's time to get her back into the real thing. I'm still feeling good about Stefan and the infinity of possibilities that have just opened up. And it really is my turn to be hung up from our little hoist. Suspended in pure bliss, your only responsibility being to ask nicely for whatever you want next. Twits writing for the *Guardian* tend to think this is abuse. Your average literary novelist might fancy it as a metaphor for fascism. Because they have no idea of what it feels like, just what it looks like.

In reality, experienced players always insist on extreme civility. Care and consideration for the other road users are top priorities.

' . . . his occult society trades on the Net worldwide. I downloaded one of their training videos!'

Her eyes are almost bulging out of her sockets. Her breath is foul as she may be starving herself again. I'm seeing more of her ribs these days than I would prefer to.

'You've got to see it!' she insists, and she's probably right. If I refuse I may well be stabbed in my sleep.

'I'm still not joining their army or whatever it is,' I tell her.

'Odin's Knot,' she says testily. I really should have remembered. 'Their symbol is the knot of the chosen.'

This is three interlocking triangles. According to them, this represents the rope that was used to dispose of sacrificial victims. On the other hand . . . 'It does look suspiciously like a swastika.'

'It represents the noose they used on their enemies,' says Sasha. 'Or the struggle to overcome that which binds us.'

'And auto-erotic asphyxiation, no doubt. Black magicians are a bit too keen on hanging as a personal development tool if you ask me.'

No one is asking me. I'm the audience. Sasha is in the chair.

'This video is an ingenious use of hypnotic conditioning,' she enthuses. 'This could hook a lot of impressionable teenagers.'

I know. I'm looking at one. But I'm no better, of course. At a stage in our relationship when other men would be sneaking out of the house to be with their mistresses I'm still under Sasha's thumb. Playing house at my age. Just because Mummy and Daddy did. But they weren't any good at it and neither are we. Sasha plugs a lead into the laptop so we can hear the soundtrack.

The video starts with an ominous low drumbeat, the sort that was sometimes provided to add a touch of gravitas to military executions. A low drone on a cheap synthesiser accompanies their swastika-like symbol rising through a red mist to glint in a most sinister fashion. I'm genuinely scared, and they haven't even started yet. The location appears to be a cheap rehearsal room. Set dressing consists entirely of their symbol in silver cardboard, some black curtains, conga drums and a microphone. A fat chap wearing army fatigues ambles into shot. He has a woollen combat mask which covers his face except for his eyes. A thin man, also wearing combat trousers and the same pierced balaclava, appears.

'It's Laurel and Hardy,' I say.

'Shush! This is lesson seven. The sigilisation of desire.'

Not that old chestnut.

'We know all this stuff,' I tell her. 'Taking a sentence which forms a wish or a spell. Rejecting any letters which repeat themselves and making a symbol out of what remains. This symbol is visualised at orgasm or at moments of great rage or hilarity, any time you can push yourself out of your normal consciousness.'

'It's never been used by Nazis before,' she says, eyes wide at the prospect of the bad boys getting hold of this powerful weapon.

'So what?'

'You know that Nazis have always used the dark energies. Right-wing esotericism is a powerful weapon that has lain dormant since the end of the Second World War. Although descendants of the Tibetan psychics who were discovered in the ruins of Berlin may still be active . . . '

'H'mm,' I say. It has always seemed to me that Hitler might have risen to power because the masses can always be united against some convenient scapegoat. Sasha thinks it's Tibetan thought-waves. I let it pass. The fat bloke's mate starts to whirl around like a dervish while playing the marracas. Sasha starts to giggle. Perhaps this is one time they shouldn't have lifted the veil on the sacred mystery. It could also be that a fat bloke with a bag on his head looks a bit silly.

'Of course, it *looks* stupid,' says Sasha, sensing that I might be about to critique some aspect of the performance. 'But you have to do it yourself. Unless you experience magic by fasting or sensual deprivation or extremes of physical deprivation you just won't get it.'

She's right – not that I'm going to let that get in my way.

'Have you ever noticed that most magickal journals seem to read something like: "swallowed some hashish, took some cocaine and laudanum, and lo and behold Baphomet appeared, accompanied by a host of cherubim and seraphim . . . " '

'Anyone can have an out-of-body experience without drugs . . . '

'Yes, it's a simple matter of sleep deprivation, endless fasting and twisting yourself into horrible contortions for days on end. Fuck that!'

'You're just lazy. In fact, we should exorcise the demon of sloth which is embedded deep inside you.'

Now, I can't say I'm entirely opposed to this, particularly

if it involves being tethered to our training trestle for some
lewd behavioural therapy. But I think she might mean trying
to keep a straight face while Sasha attempts to use her healing
hands. This means letting her cut you open with imaginary
scissors and so on. And when she's done that she spends days
in bed because she has drained off my negative energy. As if
I could ever be negative about anything.

'You need a quest! A reason to be alive! Defeating the
Dungeonmaster is exactly what you need . . . '

'What I need is a rest from the sound of your voice! You
never shut up!'

'You can't bear women to say anything at all, can you? You
just want some little housewife to bring you your pipe and
slippers.'

'That's just juvenile,' I say with a sigh.

'Well, I am juvenile compared to you. Who isn't?'

'Well, you were looking for a father figure. Now you've got
one,' I say, as I sometimes do.

'Maybe,' she mutters. 'But I don't need a grandfather figure.'

If I don't go now things will be said. Stuff that might take
weeks to get over. Or I might just get on a plane. Somewhere,
anywhere away from here. 'I need some air,' I tell her. 'I'll be
back soon.'

By the time I have mounted our cheap no-brand mountain
bike she is back rattling the keys of the laptop. But here
come green fields and the wind in my face. Neat, well-tended
pastures. Hop-fields taking a well-earned winter rest from
satisfying the locals' insatiable thirst. And no Sasha, although
her barrage of verbiage is still rattling around my head. It
takes a few steep hills and a great deal of swearing to banish
all that and then I have time to recall the events of last night

once more. Those memories – and a certain amount of lewd speculation about the near future – soon trigger mild euphoria. We can still pull! And he's right on our doorstep! He might even forget about the rent!

But then I remember Sasha's Napoleon complex. As if world domination will make up for being short. Can't she be satisfied with conquering every man she meets? Maybe that just isn't hard enough. Men give in too easily.

Perhaps this forest will calm me down. Walking along the dark tree-lined paths is like entering a cathedral was when I was a kid – a vague sense of wonder at the vastness and the scented hush. The predominant odours are of moss, damp earth and pine, a distinct improvement on the prayer books and polish you get in your average God shop. But this is the real thing, a space for quiet reflection, the chance to earth oneself. I really must make this sort of reverent pause a regular part of my life. The instant I make that decision a nearby farmer fires up some sort of industrial bone-crushing machine. It croaks and clanks, seethes and splutters. Soon it reaches a steady ratcheting and groaning rhythm that seems appropriate to a giant robot approaching some long-delayed and especially intense orgasm. Having found the right pitch – hovering just this side of a shuddering ecstatic release – the machine teases us by demonstrating its staying power, defying us to believe that something that annoying could continue for so long. It is quite insanely loud. Is it really too hard or expensive to fit some soundproofing device? Or are farmers just assumed to be dolts without a thought in their head, wholly impervious to the distress they are causing everyone within a vicinity of a mile or so? Why doesn't it bother *them*? Do they really hate the countryside that much they would want to obliterate anyone else's appreciation of it?

I shouldn't be living here. I'm just not tough enough. I need the isolation of the city. Here we have people showing up at all hours of the day and night, just because you said hello once. And have you ever tried saying hello every single time you meet anyone? Up to and including complete strangers? And here's one right now, a young woman with stray tresses of blonde hair leaking out from underneath a dark blue fleecy hat.

'Guten Tag!' she says. Well, at least that's one up on the dreaded 'Grüss Gott'. God greets you. That never fails to get on my tits. And they all say it, all the time. 'Guten Tag!' must mean she is from the Protestant north – Hamburg or Hanover.

I return her greeting in my terrible German accent.

Her face lights up. 'You're English! I thought you were German!'

She's talking broadest Lancashire. Ey up, love. The sound of my ancestral home. After all this time listening to a damned Yankee. I can't stop a smile cracking my frozen face.

'Yes. Do you live here?' I ask.

'For the moment,' she says. 'I'm Kate Lewis.'

'Matt Jackson,' I tell her, forgetting it's supposed to be a secret. 'What brings you here?'

'I'm visiting relatives. Taking a long holiday. And I'm trying to improve my German.'

'Shame the natives don't speak it then. All that bloody Bavarian.'

'I know just what you mean.' Sparkly big eyes. Warmth. What have I done to deserve all this? She certainly seems very friendly for a first meeting. And not shy about checking out the twin silver bolts in my left eyebrow; thick parallel digits that could be taken for the number eleven. But should international fugitives be wearing easily identifiable facial jewellery in the first place? However, there is only ever one question normal people pose at this point.

'Do those hurt?' she says, looking closely at my facial jewellery.

'Only while they go in,' I say.

'Are you here on holiday?'

'Sort of. We're renting part of the Bibers' farmhouse for a while.'

'Oh him! Stefan!' She mimes a man doing a Hitler salute but grabbing his arm on the way up as if trying to stop himself revealing too much. It's common shorthand in Germany to suggest that someone is a closet Nazi.

'We can't find anywhere else to live,' I tell her.

'How does your wife like it here?'

'My wife,' I say, tense and irritated again at the thought of what she is planning for us. Kate smiles sympathetically and I wonder if I have revealed too much, especially to a perfect stranger. I give my wedding ring an extra twist, to make sure it is still in place. It sometimes slips off when I dry my hands these days. It doesn't actually *mean* anything, except we should have got a smaller size, but even so . . .

'We English have to stick together,' she says, covering an awkward silence.

'Well, I don't know about that,' I tell her. 'I lived in Germany before. I don't like the sort of people who call themselves expats. The Margaret Thatcher fans. The ones who pay three quid for a copy of the *Daily Express* and hoard bottles of HP sauce.'

All my smiles are coming right back at me. If I wave a hand around, so does she. Maybe it's just a relief to talk English again. Or could there be more behind that big beaming smile? There's certainly quite a lot underneath that fleece of hers. A charming gap in her teeth, prominent chubby cheeks and big, big blue eyes. Her blonde hair is long and wayward. Not styled. She has prominent cheekbones, but they are round, curvy and nurturing. Not sharp enough to cut your fingers on. Her clothes are baggy, but it is clear that underneath lie comforting curves, nurturing rotundity. We are talking heft. Protuberance. Substance. I know men are supposed to be in awe of ten-foot-tall mop-handles, but I remain stubbornly attracted to female flesh as opposed to female bones. There is also the theory that bouncing globes of pleasantly aromatic tissue are just what is needed in a German winter − a theory that surely cries out to be put into practice as soon as possible.

Stefan might be decorative but he's not comforting. Plus, there is the moral issue of doing it with people whose politics are decidedly dodgy, something I conveniently managed to ignore last night. While gagging for it.

'Fancy a coffee?' she says. 'Or I've got some really special Darjeeling.'

She smiles as she watches me wavering. I *could* go home and carry on arguing with Sasha. Or I could find out just why I'm so attractive all of a sudden.

Kate is renting a little cottage, although hers is more modern than the frozen shack in which Sasha and I reside. She makes some Darjeeling First Flush tea, and doesn't even mind when I seize a pile of recent English newspapers. 'You're homesick,' she says, watching me riffle through these otherwise terminally tedious items.

'Maybe,' I concede.

She scurries over to her PC, where a stack of e-mail is waiting for her. Once she's dealt with that she skins up while chatting cheerily about what brought her to the middle of nowhere.

She worked in television until some treachery on the part of a colleague led to her being dumped. Then her marriage collapsed. It's disloyal to tell her about what a pain Sasha's being, but I have asked her nicely about a million times not to get us killed. And she just won't listen. Kate seems rather good at that underrated skill, and several hours pass while we exchange personal histories. These may well be carefully edited – mine certainly is – but just hearing an English voice again is enough to drive me wild with desire. I don't know why a northern English accent should be any more erotic than an American one, but it seems more . . . homely? Have I honestly been reduced to that? I suppose the not-killing-people thing would have to be another reason as to why she is so alluring. She wouldn't have to be dissuaded from forming a gang and storming a neo-Nazi castle. Kate wouldn't want to do that in the first place.

By the time the dope is starting to take effect she has put Anita Baker's 'Rapture' on, just as it's dark enough to light some candles. Hearing these mellow grooves again is like slipping into a warm scented bath, all the more welcome for being unexpected. I have got used to frazzling my nerves with Sasha's collection of art-school rubbish. She usually wants to listen to whatever will be out of date by the time anyone else has heard of it. Even better, it should be so abrasive that it will remain forever marginal. Anita Baker was never fashionable. It just sounded nice. And hit a chord with people at the start of relationships. It went well with lovemaking and premium ice-cream. It was soppy and gooey and girls like me liked it. And now, thanks to Kate, I can hear it all again – even while trapped in the coldest, bleakest place on earth.

'That's lovely,' I say.

'Good,' she replies.

'Oooh!' she says, tugging her boots off and kneading her feet. She looks a little sheepish when she sees my raised eyebrows. 'Sorry. I walked for miles and miles today.'

And once she has thrown her red socks away I can see that she paints her toenails purple. Today's ramblers seem rather different from the ones I remember as a sullen teenager, desperate to escape my parents' endless exploration of the Peak District.

'I could rub your feet,' I say, knowing I shouldn't. But striking lucky with Stefan must have made me reckless.

'You don't want to go anywhere near *those*!' she says, quite inaccurately as it happens. Feet are one of my favourite bits. And always a reliable icebreaker. Although it always starts with a woman saying, 'Oh no, you won't want to do that.' After another token show of resistance from Kate I soon have her feet propped up on my thighs. Gently rubbing my knuckles around the soles of her feet elicits a deep groan from her and then she is gone, lost, drifting somewhere in space.

Her feet are at the mozzarella end of the olfactory spectrum, although I wouldn't have minded if they had been closer to Stilton. In fact, it's hard not to continue the massage with lips and tongue but I somehow manage to keep some control of myself. Not that it's easy, what with her moaning and groaning and the gentle undulation of her breasts every time she shifts position.

Our chemistry seems just right. Soon her breathing has deepened and her mouth is open. I could rub her ankles and then proceed slowly onwards and upwards. Another five minutes of mellifluous Anita Baker and we will be caught up in the rapture of Kate's thighs. Perhaps they are too muscular for some screaming queen of a fashion designer, but they are exactly the sort of tactile delight that sets warm blood gently seeping into erectile tissue. Even before we have got anywhere near them. It *is* hot in here. And her warm breath smells nice. Ten minutes from now it wouldn't be so inappropriate to cup the cheeks of her bottom in my hands while dipping my face down to what some heathens call 'the great gate'. Sasha's not fond of that expression, although she needn't worry, being petite and perfectly formed.

Kate. Cute, kissable Kate. And this might even be a way of having sex without having to kill people. With any luck. Or will Sasha crawl through the door, knife between her gleaming teeth, and cut both our hearts out? Why am I even thinking about hearts? Has a recent taste for cross-dressing turned me into a real girl? I'll be worried about my weight next. I might start to care about the tragic death of Princess Diana. I might send a small proportion of my income to help donkeys escape ritual death in Spain. I'm even worried about betraying my partner. I just can't do any of this, not while Sasha's stern face is in front of me, wagging an admonitory finger. Kate opens her eyes.

'What's the matter?' she says.

'I'm sorry. I feel awkward. Being married.'

It didn't stop us last night with Stefan, of course, but Kate is a civilian. Not a professional.

'It's an open relationship but . . . I would have to tell Sasha. My wife.'

'Will she scratch my eyes out?' she says, smiling broadly once more. The ease with which she says this would seem to indicate that she may be familiar with crumbling relationships and broken crockery. She is thirty-something, divorced and quite possibly the veteran of countless disastrous relationships and one-night stands. I just don't know. And the dope has made me much too paranoid to make any such judgements anyway.

'I'm sorry. I'd better go. We had an argument. It needs fixing before anything else can happen. I'm sorry.'

She nods slowly. 'Come over again,' she says. 'For a chat.'

'I'd love to. It's just that . . . '

'Don't worry! I'd love to see you again. When you can think straight. Go on! Go home and patch it up!'

There was a time when reviewers wrote dismissively of novels which featured adultery in Hampstead. I don't know whether betrayal hurts any less in Hampstead, but I would suspect the answer is that it doesn't. Once discovered, it has the potential to poison every single memory retrospectively. So the injured person is robbed of their past as well as whatever future they thought they had. Even when you are allowed to commit adultery, as Sasha and I both are, it still hurts. As does not committing adultery. So you might as well get stuck in and worry about it later. Not that there is any choice in the matter. Shakespeare might have put it slightly better in the Sonnets: ''Tis better to be vile than vile esteemed when not to be receives reproach of being.'

Which is a lovely turn of phrase. But then he never had to cope with his primary partner insisting that he should spend weeks on end crawling around the floor dressed as a schoolgirl. In a blonde pigtailed wig that doesn't *really* fit, whatever Sasha says. This polyamorous lifestyle is supposed to be fine if you can define the rules. Unfortunately, the Great Mother seems to have decreed that nothing is any fun unless it involves breaking the rules. Maybe it's not the right time to tell Sasha about this latest development.

'What are you looking so pleased about?' says Sasha, as I return with some of her favourite chocolates. She'll find out. So I might as well throw myself on her mercy.

'I met an English woman. In the forest. She's quite a laugh actually.'

Sasha now looks as if she will never smile again.

'I've only just met her,' I say.

Time freezes. We both know. Something has happened. Cupid has fired one of his little arrows and it's stuck right in my heart.

'Well, if she's all sweet and cute maybe you should go for it,' says Sasha. 'I'm obviously too much trouble.'

Before I can stop myself, some sort of agreement with that last statement must have flickered over my face.

'Most men want an angel at home and a bad girl for a mistress,' says Sasha. 'You seem to be the other way around.'

'Perhaps that's what I'm doing wrong,' I say. 'I'm not actually up to living with a bad girl.' Sorry if that's a bit obvious, but I've only just noticed. After seven years.

'She's welcome to you,' says Sasha.

'We only just said hello. Shall we keep the divorce papers on hold? Anyway, she started it.'

Sasha hides her lovely face behind her hands while waiting for the last stray giggles to cease bubbling their way through her. Anyone who wasn't me would find the sight enchanting. But I know she's trying to annoy me.

'I'm sorry,' she says. 'But you don't have to pretend it's her fault. You can even shag her if you want. I don't care.'

Which is a new one. Surely she can't be falling for Stefan. So he's gorgeous. So he's a millionaire. So what? I'm a trustworthy loyal mongrel. What use is his pedigree good looks and bulging bank account against that?

Her bright cheery face nods a few times. Go on. Fill your boots, it seems to be saying. But why? Can't she even pretend to be jealous? As far as I could gather from stuff she used to say, I am the finest male specimen presently available and, even though she could have anyone, I should be honoured that she has decided to devote her life to me. Can't she pretend to be upset?

'I don't want to shag her,' I say, before being unable to continue because of Sasha's baleful glare. 'Well, I might. A bit.'

'Remember asking me to stop having sex with other people? Last year?'

'Well, I was a bit upset at the time. What with all those people dying around us.'

'You could at least have asked me to join in. Like with Stefan.'

Sasha's usual attitude to any new partners I might have is to sleep with the person in question, then have better sex with them. She will then embark on a longer, even messier entanglement, during which I will have ample time to catch up on my light reading. Then we are back together again, usually cheered by the fact that we are less awful than whoever the new thrill was.

But the problem with all this polyamorous stuff is that you are supposed to have a post-mortem with your primary partner. You also have to set an unbelievable number of rules and regulations before you can even start. Then you are supposed to confess every time you transgress. Very soon you start to long for the old system of clandestine affairs, visits to sex workers and, perhaps best of all, a tantric love affair with oneself. Gliding along on a succession of spermless orgasms.

'You can enjoy this . . . person,' says Sasha, smiling serenely, 'if you want. I know I've been a bit busy, tracking down the Dungeonmaster. Working on the Brotherhood of Saturn documents. Stefan said he would help me forge them. The Dungeonmaster would probably pay a fortune for them.'

'We are supposed to be in hiding,' I point out. 'Fugitives. And not appearing on primetime chat shows.' Which is Sasha's real goal, whatever she actually says or does.

'Stefan and I know what to write,' she says. 'Then we just need some pre-war stationery and ink. And some tame forger.'

Unfortunately, I have a hard skull. If I hammer my head against our stone walls it is still not possible for me to dash my brains out.

'The more people you involve the more likely it is to go wrong.'

'Not if you ask people nicely,' says Sasha. She grins winningly. After a lifetime of wrapping men around her little finger I suppose she thinks it's a foregone conclusion. She might be right, actually.

' . . . if an amateur forger managed to convince the *Sunday Times* and some historians that Hitler's diaries existed . . . why shouldn't we be able to forge a membership document two pages long which proves that Hitler was initiated into an occult society which still exists? Aleister Crowley was in the same society. Twenty years later but . . . it would be worth a fortune.'

It would. How on earth can I put her off? Pretend to go along for a while, perhaps. Or try appealing to her sense of morality.

'Crowley was a user. He destroyed most of his lovers. He was nasty and vicious while pretending to be all submissive . . .'

'Like you . . .'

'. . . and he was anti-semitic. Much more than he needed to be by the standards of the time. He was also a traitor who worked for the German secret service, supposedly directing them to bomb his auntie's home or some such wizard wheeze.'

'I never liked his "jokes",' says Sasha.

'Yeah. He thought he was a much better poet than Shakespeare. Or so he said. Perhaps that was another one of his rib-ticklers. But he certainly left his mark. Most of what he popularised is now available in high-street bookshops. Astrology, yoga, kinky sex, drugs. Mysticism in general. It's all down to Uncle Aleister. The anal sex doesn't seem to have caught on . . . '

'. . . it has round here,' Sasha reminds me with a pointed look.

'Yes, well, if we could tie Hitler in with one of these occult initiation ceremonies . . . '

'. . . Something to do with bondage and whipping . . . '

'. . . as they usually are. This would be a hot story.'

Unfortunately, I seem to have talked myself around to her point of view. But she might be right. Hitler is always good box office.

'Aren't we supposed to be in hiding?' I say.

'What are they going to do? Arrest us for forgery?'

'It has been known. In fact, it's quite likely.'

Even though this latest plan rings alarm bells, I still don't have the courage to leave. She knows I'm not going anywhere. She is the boss. The champion of champions. Probably because she is the only one who can be bothered to listen to what I say. That's why she has no need to fear whatever Kate, 'this person', might have to offer. Who else would put up with me?

'You've got some post,' she says, tossing me over a package. 'Looks like a book.'

'It'll be *Who Killed Rob Powers?*' I tell her, a piece of junk I ordered off the Internet. And so it is. We are not in the index so I throw it in the corner. Rob Powers was a rock star client of Sasha's, now tragically deceased. Someone or other, most probably secret service buddies of her father's, cleared up the mess then dumped his body in the Hudson River. Unfortunately, it floated to the surface, just like other waste products that sometimes bob up however often you flush.

We made a cable show shortly before he vanished from sight, and one young man with no friends has started to post messages pointing out that Sasha and I seem to have disappeared too. No one really cares about conspiracy theories cooked up by Rob Powers' fans, but we really should be pottering about in the countryside – hellishly boring though it is – rather than causing any more trouble. Rob's autopsy said suicide. Which it was. Unfortunately, Rob's fans tend to think, 'He couldn't have left us like this! It must have been murder!'

So Rob's cult is still growing. He's not quite up there with Jim Morrison, a clutch of recent rappers or dear Diana, who may eventually outlast most other goddesses. But Rob is now a rock god, although his place in the pantheon is presently the subject of much debate. Could he have saved a whole generation, like the blessed Kurt Cobain? Was he as great a musician as Sid Vicious or this week's dead 'gangstas'? How will we ever get over the early demise of rappers whose only skill is encouraging kids to shoot each other? Meanwhile, the tills are ringing. Anyone with a piece of Rob Powers is richer than they used to be.

'It might even be worth selling our rehearsal tapes,' says Sasha.

'We can't break cover just for a few grand!'

'We auction them, numb-nuts. Sorry, I'm just not sleeping.'

Again. And soon we will be in that time of the month when strong men tremble. As I am not a particularly strong man, you can imagine the effect Sasha's PMT has on me. Sasha once called me a Nazi because I wanted to move out for three days every month. Unfortunately, she never knows which three days it is so we have to struggle on. 'You're mad all the time,' she tends to say. 'Every time you're hungry. Every time you're coming off drugs. And every time you drink too much coffee.' And I tend to change the subject.

'Actually there *is* something you might be right about. We *are* being stalked on the Net again.'

'The cookie monster?'

This was Sasha's phrase for the devices that follow your progress around the Net. It's usually done to target you for goods and services, but it's not completely impossible that someone could examine every single Rob Powers' nut who follows the conspiracy theories. With a view to tracking down the mystery couple who were so cruel to poor old Rob on a cable show just before he vanished.

'Did you know Rob's mom posted a reward to get his killers?'

'I didn't. And I can't say it's cheered me up particularly.

'She has millions to spend. And nothing to do now the light of her life is dead.'

And meanwhile there are clubs in London and Amsterdam where people queue up to gratify our every sexual whim. And now I've found out how to get real Ecstasy, even I can have a good time. But I'm stuck here. Where it's cold and grey. With the clinically insane.

'You see, we might even be safer chasing the Dungeonmaster . . . if someone is tracking us down,' says Sasha.

In an attempt to distract her from this hare-brained scheme I start rubbing my body against hers. And then slow dancing with one of her veils. *That's* how desperate I am to distract her.

'You should do it professionally,' says Sasha. 'You'd be so good. With your cute little butt wiggling along to the music.'

I smile weakly. It's nice to know that at least one part of me is flawless. I don't know why I don't just graft my entire arse over where my face presently is and present *that* to the world. It has to be some sort of improvement over what the world usually gets to see – an Aleister Crowley lookalike with teeth as cracked and crooked as the Conservative shadow cabinet. Whoever they may be. My mum told me that if I didn't smile my face would stick like that. And how right she has turned out to be.

'Do me,' I tell her, licking and nuzzling her bare toes. She's standing up, I'm kneeling at her feet. You would think she would be happy with this state of affairs but apparently not.

'No!' she says. 'You do *me*. I want to be the centre of attention for a change.'

I was once punched in the stomach and couldn't breathe for a while. That last statement has had a surprisingly similar effect.

'Don't look like that,' she says, wagging a finger at me. 'You're so needy! Whatever I give you is never enough!'

'That's ridiculous.'

'You just want to be fisted again.'

I get to my feet. I'm not going to take that from anyone. Unfortunately. ' "When Two Switches Both Want To Sub",' I say, thinking of the hours of fun she could have with that one on the Internet. 'How do you decide? Toss a coin.'

'It should just happen,' she says.

'And nasty horrid men should stop torturing little kittens for profit. But they probably won't,' I say. I really shouldn't have said that. Especially as it gets her back on the subject of the Dungeonmaster.

'We have to stop the Dungeonmaster and his vivisectionist friends!' she says, eyes ablaze.

'Yes! We will. But we also need to stop working occasionally.'

'We?'

'Never mind. I'll go out on the mountain bike.'

That stops her. The ghost of Kate materialises before Sasha banishes her with a twisted little smile.

'All right.' She puts our laptop on standby mode with one last wistful click of the mouse. 'Come here.'

'Don't stop,' she says an hour later. Well, that's easy for her to say. I'm a bit tuckered out.

'If you want to carry on you'll have to strap Marvin on,' I say. That's what we call our biggest, blackest dildo. The one that does the sexual healing.

'You're *such* a slut,' she says, with enough affection to bring a fond smile to my face.

'It's *you*,' I tell her. 'You make me do it.'

'If that helps, use it.'

'Come on!' I tell her, a tad miffed that she can't reciprocate for everything I've just done. What is this? Slave labour?

'Do it!' I tell her, starting to worry her leg like a frisky Jack Russell.

Sasha gets Marvin and straps it on to her favourite harness.

Soon I know what it's like to be a woman as she slops some lube on, not bothering about warming it up or how rough she's being. And then some clumsy thrusts miss their mark. It's cute watching her tongue loll out of her mouth as she takes aim, though. And then . . . suddenly. Good. Golly. Miss. Molly. That *is* a big one. But it's doable. And Sasha likes the reverse thrust effect. Something or other is making her grunt like a hog. Some further swinishness ensues. To our mutual benefit, as we drift slowly on and up. Soon most of my body feels like it's full of warm champagne. The wife's looking perky too.

'Ooh baby,' she says. And I can't disagree. I feel quite giddy.

Then the phone rings. Sasha's such a career girl that she just has to stop to listen to whoever it is on the answerphone. I wish she hadn't, though. For it is her long-lost auntie. As far as I knew she had cut her family off.

'Sasha. I have bad news. Your mother is very ill. There really isn't much time left. I know there have been some problems but . . . please call her.'

There's a sob in her voice. Sorrow floods my body and my dormant tear ducts start to fill up. I wasn't close to the old bat, both old bats if you want to include her auntie, but I'm thinking of what the effect will be on Sasha. And the way family bereavement hit me. Sasha disengages, which is only right really.

'Please call her,' says Auntie Joan.

Sasha looks at me. As if I could help with this or anything else.

'You'd better call her,' I say softly. And she nods.

5

'I WANT TO go home for Xmas!' I tell Sasha.

'We have no home,' she says. She spent some hours talking to her mum last night. Long enough to heal some wounds. Long enough to put the FBI on our trail also. Sasha made a vague promise to try to get there, but I have no way of knowing whether she will go. I dragged Stefan in here to distract her.

And he was only too pleased to oblige, crawling in naked with a freshly cut birch between his teeth. She gives Stefan's bare bum a few licks with this implement, which has been lovingly soaked and tied up in red ribbon. Stefan begged her to soak it in her wee, but she refused. He's had to make do with mine, but he seems happy enough. Down there on the cold stone floor. His arms have been trussed up behind him, which is apparently more appropriate for those who like to play pony games. I couldn't care less about any of that but who hasn't dreamed of tying their landlord up and subjecting him to a series of humiliating tortures? The only problem with all this is that Stefan wants us to do it. Sasha will get no revelations about the Dungeonmaster out of him however spitefully she uses that birch. Although we have been offered two first-class tickets to London and some accommodation with a view of the river. Problem is, he wants to come too. Sasha wants a few more concessions first. As if free first-class air travel and a place to stay isn't enough.

'Tell us about the tournament!' says Sasha.

She's wearing a white silk shirt, black jodhpurs and knee-length boots. He shakes his head. He may not know. Or he may want more punishment. I don't mind either way. There's nothing much on the telly.

'Right,' says Sasha. And she appears to be genuinely annoyed.

'On your back.'

She sits down firmly on his head and clamps her thighs tightly around him. His erection swells to bursting point as she rocks on his face. It's hard for Stefan to breathe right now. But there are worse ways to go.

She winks at me as she opens her copy of the *Meditations* of Marcus Aurelius. She has recently been trying to get me to be a little more stoic. And moan a little less.

'Listen to this,' she says. 'He's talking about "those who waste their time with bitter reviling".' She has raised her eyebrows and is staring directly at me with a fixed smile.

'Are you trying to tell me something?' I ask her.

She spins the book gently and carefully into my lap. 'Read it!' she says.

Well, I can't let that pass. This idea that she might know something that I don't. Especially as this wisdom exists in the form of a Penguin Classic and is therefore part of my cultural heritage – whether I've read it or not – as opposed to some Mickey Mouse stuff Sasha might know.

'So what if he was always right?' I say. 'He still looks like Jerry Hayes.'

There are some mute whinnies of protest from Stefan, and a yelp as she uses the birch directly on his erection. I'll bet that would make even Marcus Aurelius's eyes water. I study the Penguin edition, the cover of which features a bust designed to immortalise the great man. It does indeed look as if one of the wisest men who has ever lived looks uncomfortably like one of the silliest.

'Who *is* Jerry Hayes?' she says. She looks worried, as if there might be some important artist or political figure that it would be shameful not to have heard of.

'You know,' I tell her, 'the blond curly-haired ringpiece who used to be on the James Whale show.'

Sasha's been on it and she still can't remember.

'Marcus Aurelius is an asshole? Because two thousand years later some idiot bears a slight resemblance to him?' says Sasha shamingly. 'How pathetic is *that*?'

Which is typical. When I try to bond with her by suggesting that hairstyles and surface sheen are more important than anything else, she immediately becomes a grey-bearded professor of logic.

Sasha runs the tip of her fingernail up Stefan's shaft. His heels start to drum on the floor until she suddenly grabs his scrotum and squeezes hard. 'Keep still! And no coming until we tell you!'

Sasha smiles at me. Do continue, she seems to be saying.

'I'm just saying all achievement is transient,' I say, summarising a paragraph I've just read for the first time. 'As Marcus said.'

'So it's *Marcus* now. I wonder what his female slaves were doing while he was sat on his ass cogitating.'

'Probably building a perfect non-heirarchical society,' I say. 'They certainly wouldn't have been scratching each other's eyes out and making endless bitchy remarks behind each other's backs.'

'You would be *so* good as a girl.'

'I *am* so good as a girl,' I remind her. Even if I am finding it hard to maintain a credible female wardrobe on the pittance she gives me.

'You're a good slut,' she admits. 'But men always dress up as tarts. They have no idea of style.'

And then the bells start again. It's almost enough to make you go native. And resort to beer. But Sasha and I must never drink. It's way too dangerous. As is amateur detection – not that there is any chance of keeping Sasha to this one. She does like poking her nose in where it is not required. But for the moment it is Stefan's snout which is firmly in the trough. And it really should be mine. I wonder if Sasha is getting an extra thrill from showing me that I'm not the only man who likes worshipping her. Or whether it is his hot breath which is getting to her. Or the feel of his nose and mouth as she presses the seat of her pants all over his face. They are both gasping as the scene seems to be close to some sort of resolution.

But suddenly Sasha's weeping. The scene wasn't enough to make her forget about her mum. I go over and hug her until it stops while Stefan stays still and mute underneath her. Even he's helping in his own small way. Although he stays inappropriately hard while I'm comforting Sasha.

'Sorry, babe,' I tell her, wondering what on earth you can ever say at times like this. We sit together on the couch for a while. Stefan stays perfectly still, his hard-on gently deflating.

Eventually Sasha pulls herself together and orders him to crouch at our side.

'Not like that! Get your butt up!'

Handing out a fresh thrashing seems to restore her equilibrium, but I've seen her in better spirits. I might not be the right person to say this but I think she's dangerously unstable presently. She just won't eat. And that will send you mad quicker than just living with me.

When it's over and Stefan has thanked her profusely he is allowed to bring us in some fresh coffee. This sees him back in ponyboy costume, saddled up with a cute swishy little tail protruding from his reddened bottom. He has braided some red ribbons into this tail. They almost match my boots. It seems appropriate to give him a sugar cube. He laps this up, flirting with me from under his floppy quiff as he does so.

'I have a large flat,' he then tells us, not for the first time that day. 'On the river. You will show me London and I will show you the Dungeonmaster. It is decided.'

Sasha and I exchange a glance. After all that has just transpired he is still trying to give us orders. But that's slaves for you. You'd get more deference from a London cabbie than from the average devoted slave. Sasha gives him a vicious slash with her crop. It lands on the back of his thighs. Where it hurts. There is a genuine cry of pain which Stefan soon converts to a whinny and a shake of his head.

'*We* have decided,' says Sasha. 'Master Matt and Mistress Sasha.'

Personally, I find such titles restrictive to the free flow of passion and pervery. But if it gets us an acquiescent millionaire with an open wallet I'm happy to play along.

'Kiss Matt's feet,' says Sasha.

He scampers over and covers my shiny red boots with hot

sweet kisses. I can feel his breath warm my ankles and calves. It should feel better than it does, having this delightful creature working so hard to please me. But the pleasure is slightly muted by the knowledge that Sasha is attempting to manipulate me presently. The eternal conflict between us still rages. But there's the view of a slender devoted slave at my feet. My hard-working little pony. And, better than anything else, Sasha's smile. She's happy right now. And triggering that ever-elusive state is probably what I was put here to do. *My* destiny.

'You won't be able to see Kate in London,' says Sasha, smiling sweetly.

I shrug as if I don't care. And why should I? Having already arranged to meet her there.

6

THE GNOSTIC MASS was adapted into the 'Great Rite' of modern witchcraft. That Wicca normally involves nudity and copulation, bondage and scourging has led some cynics to doubt whether it is practised for wholly religious motives.

Sex Magic for Today by Jocelyn Chaplin and Gareth J. Medway

Stefan's riverside flat is between Tower Bridge and London Bridge – an area containing several tourist-friendly medieval torture chambers and more than a few dungeons not open to the general public. This may be why the doorman looks up sharply when Sasha announces we are staying at number 210. There's something hovering around the edges of his not-so-servile smile. And it isn't just the traditional British rudeness in service industries.

'What have you been up to?' Sasha asks Stefan as we take the lift.

'I used some prostitutes—'

'—sex workers!' says Sasha, rightly so.

'Sex workers,' says Stefan, with a mutinous little twitch of the eyebrows. 'So-called dominant women,' he says. 'They were useless. I could speak better English than many of them. How could they dominate *me*?'

'And I thought it was just the English who were snobs,' says Sasha for my benefit. A wise man would say nothing. I open my mouth.

'I just said, once, as an opinion, that "domination" sounds better in English. To some people, it just doesn't sound as good in American. Or in Birmingham or whatever . . . ' I look at Stefan, hoping he will agree.

'You are definitely a nationalist,' he says to me. 'Stop fighting it. And why be ashamed anyway? What is wrong with celebrating your own language and your own people? Or are white people the only ones who aren't allowed national pride?'

'The Nazis were corporate buttheads,' I tell him. 'So are nationalists. I'm an individual.'

Sasha gives me a sharp look, the meaning of which escapes me for a moment. Then I remember we are supposed to be on Stefan's side. I have stepped out of my role yet again.

'Sorry, Stefan,' I tell him. 'I never did like taking orders. Maybe the Black Order isn't for me.'

'You take orders from me,' chimes in Sasha.

But before I can chide her for that, Stefan has let us into the flat. Sasha is soon doing her special cheerleader dance. The flat is heart-rendingly cute. And who wouldn't be happy after the cold stone shack we have been living in? There's warmth and opulence and two white leather sofas. The view's not bad either; St Paul's and the City.

But Sasha isn't going to stand for Stefan's taste in sculpture and painting. As you can tell what some of Stefan's paintings are supposed to be, they must be rubbish – in Sasha's view.

Or they should have been any old crud on video or an ironic pastiche of something – the usual excuse the talentless offer. I couldn't possibly be clever enough to understand art so I head straight for one of the big white leather couches.

Once I have spread myself all over that I can check out Stefan's books. He has a fine occult selection, including an entire shelf of possibly speculative opinion regarding Hitler's youthful dabbling with the occult. It remains open to question whether various shadowy sorcerers were required to help Hitler spread racial hatred among the masses – not a difficult task then or now.

Stefan has a well-read copy of *The Spear of Destiny* by Trevor Ravenscroft, which remains the market leader in this field. His son Raphael played the saxophone solo on Gerry Rafferty's 'Baker Street', information I never previously found a use for.

'You don't believe all this crap, do you?' I ask Stefan, holding up the book, which has mad scribbles all over it.

'But of course!' he says, laughing at my ignorance. 'There is no doubt that Hitler was initiated into the darkest mysteries! How could he have achieved so much without the assistance of some extra-terrestrial force helping him?'

'Wasn't it just killing anyone who disagreed with him?'

'No. No. No. He used force where it was necessary . . . '

'What?'

'He used force *where it was necessary*,' repeats Stefan, rather surprised I'm disagreeing with him. Sasha flashes me another look. The one that means 'Don't say anything ever again. Or at least not for the next few moments.'

'And why not?' says Stefan, extending a hand to include me in his next statement. 'We Germans are natural warriors,'

'I'm not German . . . ' I say, but no one's listening.

'You are Germanic,' he says. 'Of Nordic descent. Tacitus points out that the German people are naturally warlike. In the first century AD.'

'We say CE now. Common era,' insists Sasha. 'It takes Christ out of it.'

'What does it matter if we mention Christ in passing?' says Stefan. 'You're too dogmatic! All your rules and regulations!'

Sasha can't speak for a moment. I suppose it must be annoying being told you're a control freak by a card-carrying Nazi. Or nationalist, as Stefan usually insists.

'Besides, YF is used among the elite. Year after the Führer's birth . . . '

But Sasha's attention has drifted. She has seen something hideous. Her blood is up. 'What's that?' she says, clearly incensed. She's pointing at a life-size silver greyhound.

'I got it from a gallery in Mayfair,' says Stefan, ice cool in the face of her derisive laugh.

'You bought that?' she asks, aghast that some art has been produced using hand-to-eye coordination and other arcane skills – and this ten years after she personally decreed that such things should never happen again. I don't like it because it conjures up a large hound with alarmingly lifelike genitals. In my own admittedly untrained view, the fewer dogs' dicks there are in a work of art the better.

'And don't you start!' says Sasha, although I had no intention of doing so.

The last time we discussed art, Sasha pointed out that the only political party to mirror my own hatred of the contemporary product is Jorg Haider's Freedom Party. Which was slightly unsettling. But whether the cutting of huge grants to Austrian conceptualists is fascism or merely sound government remains open to debate. And one day I'll say that to Sasha. I will.

But rather than cause any more trouble I make a call to Luke, an old friend who sells genuine Ecstasy. No speed, no aspirin – just the love stuff. I'm keen to feel loved up again. And even keener to get Sasha surfing the universal love wave again. A few days of that and she will soon forget recruiting her noble knights. You mark my words.

'What a great view of St Paul's,' says Sasha, walking towards the window.

'Don't open it!' says Stefan. 'There are many flies! It's the river. At low tide.'

So the dream house on the river fills up with flies. Yet another delusion mercilessly skewered. And it's noisy here. Even with the window shut we can hear several different car alarms and some serious demolition work with jackhammers but, however hard you listen, you can't hear church bells. And that's music to my ears. Or it would be if Stefan wasn't talking.

'We must go out. It is the weekend!'

As if it mattered what day normal people get drunk.

'I want to find Jamie,' says Sasha. 'He will be just right for this mission. He does a street show in town. We could all go together.'

'Not while there's breath in my body,' I tell her, standing up to add weight to my objections.

'You're coming,' she says, without looking at me. 'And you, Stefan. You'll love the British buskers. They're *radical*.'

'Yes. This will be most entertaining,' says Stefan without irony. 'But you really *must* take me to a fetish party.'

I don't know. He seems to think that, just because he's paying us, he's in charge, rather than the other way around. But it is not yet time to make Stefan see the error of his

ways. For the moment we must be content thinking up mou-
thwatering tortures to practise on him. I favour a Native
American technique of wrapping him in a wet animal skin
that will gradually tighten over a few days or so. It is slow
but certain. Sasha thinks we should put him in the animal
skin and then leave him in a home-improvement centre on a
bank holiday. Let him listen to families bickering and Muzak
as he chokes out his last breath. But that would be sadistic.
Not the sort of consensual behaviour Sasha and I insist on
with our playmates. Mind you, if he says I'm German one
more time . . .

'I hope you will arrange something a little special for me,'
says Stefan, a remark that could probably have done with a
bit more deference.

Sasha just smiles enigmatically. He remains unaware that
she might carve her initials in his face sometime soon.

'Let me make a few phone calls,' she says in a very quiet
girlie voice.

Now the little woman has left us, Stefan offers me a drink.
He throws open the doors of a very well-stocked cocktail
cabinet. Inside there is everything Jay Gatsby might have
needed for a drink and everything that has been invented
since. It's even lit from the inside to flatter the comprehensive
selection of spirits, mixers, shakers and every type of cocktail
glass ever invented. I know I shouldn't but I start to read the
labels. I can almost hear the sweet sickly liqueurs whispering
to me: 'Go on! Have a drink, mate! You haven't killed anyone
for ages! You're cured! Go *on*!' Several bottles of twelve-year-
old single malt kid me that I have recovered enough to let
their smooth elegance seep over my palate. As if I wouldn't
still wake up in jail three days later, perhaps not even in
England. A bottle of Pernod lifts its skirt and winks at me. I

can almost smell her cool aniseed breath, feel her busy hands firmly overcome my token resistance.

'I learned some interesting cocktails on my last visit . . .' says Stefan.

'I'll make some tea,' I tell him, rather than grab his lapels and launch my forehead at his delicate little nose.

'Tea!' he says, smiling enthusiastically again. 'Tea in England! You must show me how you make it!'

There is not a hint of irony. He genuinely wants to know. He scampers off to a cabinet and presents me with a packet of Winston Churchill tea just as Sasha returns.

'Cool! Let's have some tea!' she says, enthused at the prospect.

'Why don't we go and watch the changing of the guard while we're at it?' I say, but the two tourists want to have a tea party. Sasha takes charge, just for a change, so I go and have a quick mutter over by the window.

'There's a private party tomorrow,' says Sasha. 'But we mustn't say anything about politics. Not a hint of our true beliefs.'

'Why be shy?' asks Stefan, grinning broadly. 'We are winning the argument now. You have Romanian Gypsies roaming your suburbs . . . and your papers are coming round to our views.'

He brandishes a copy of a mid-market tabloid left over from his last visit. This one was supporting Oswald Mosley's blackshirts in the 1930s and is now full of asylum-seeker scare stories. It is mostly read by women, who don't seem to mind being told that single mothers are an evil menace, not if there are adequate amounts of astrology and shopping. And condensed versions of the classics – *Bridget Jones, Love Lives of the Royal and Famous*, *How to Lose Weight* by Any Woman Who's Been On The Telly recently.

'Don't ever carry that thing near me,' says Sasha, batting the thing away from her with frantically waving hands. 'I'll stop your training!'

'Maybe I will find a new trainer,' says Stefan, taunting Sasha ever so gently. 'There are many near here.'

And so there are. It's just handy for the City. Those nasty little boys who shout into phones all day like a bit of that. Corrective training. Personality modification. Invasive procedures. You can do anything to that lot. Except whisper in their ear why they like their male bonding so much. There are some things even they won't joke about.

Stefan is shuffling his pack of phone cards advertising the local sex workers.

'Let's have a look,' says Sasha, grabbing the cards out of his hands. 'Is *she* still at it? And I thought necrophilia was illegal.'

'Who's that?' I say, always eager for a bit of gossip.

'It's "Old Cold Cathy". "Mature model?" You said it, babe.

'That's not helpful, dear,' I say. 'What happened to sexual diversity?'

'Yeah. But no children, no animals and no cadavers. So no Cathy.'

'Sasha!'

'Wow! Look at this!' she says, waving a phone card at me. 'It's us!'

And so it is. Some struggling artiste has scanned an old picture of Sasha and me. Many would take offence at this blatant theft, but Sasha will just take it back to the kiosk and ensure that it gets the best possible placing. Even in a phone box she would insist on top billing. And we do look nice. My face is mercifully blurred, but there is plenty of space devoted to the only photogenic bit of my body – my arse.

'You've got such a lovely little butt,' says Sasha as I show her the card.

'Do you think so? I never liked that shot. There are better angles . . .'

'Listen to you! You little slut!'

She tousles some imaginary hair, or the real hair I used to have. Perhaps she's massaging my aura again. If you've never had this service, just try and imagine someone nearly stroking your forehead with their fingers. It's almost indistinguishable from the real thing.

Even Sasha can't handle going out tonight. The agony will start tomorrow, when I will be dragged around central London to listen to a lot of buskers. It's a situation that calls for heroin. But the only non-alcoholic mood-altering substance available is Winston Churchill tea. I take a cup of the tepid stewed brew and use it to numb myself as Sasha tells me her plans.

Waking up in London with a view of the river should be idyllic. But the sound of Sasha tapping away at her laptop reminds me that we have a mission. We are not here just to enjoy ourselves. Oh no. Today's quest is especially hazardous. We are to ask every street entertainer we can find if they know what became of Jamie Gee, a kilted animal-rights fanatic. According to Sasha, he is an ex-services man who became an eco-warrior after his first acid trip. He then travelled to the States to be hung by his tits off a tree by some Native Americans. During two days spent swinging from a giant redwood he experienced many visions, chief among which was the sight of a giant McDonald's sign. They won't let them eat or drink while this is happening, you know. But all you come out of it with is the ability to say things like 'We are all one', 'We must save the planet'. And some lovely scars where the hooks went.

Sasha seems to think all this is rather glamorous. As if I couldn't have fought in the Falklands war if I had wanted to. Or learned sword-making or falconry or judo or . . . I'm getting rather tired of Jamie and we haven't even met yet.

If this wasn't enough, he is apparently a crack shot and a lethal exponent of the accordion. He is said to carry a tin whistle to play jigs and reels on, and there are unconfirmed reports that he possesses a set of bagpipes. If this is so, I'm turning myself in. Satanic Nazis are one thing; Celtic pipers are quite another.

'Can't you just look him up on the Internet?' I ask her as we shoulder our way through Soho, dodging drunks and drug addicts rattling their collecting cups at us.

'Jamie hates the Net,' says Sasha. 'He likes to live in the past. Like you.'

Her smile is affectionate. And she couldn't hear any reply I might make anyway as we are now listening to some street entertainers who have thoughtfully brought a full-strength amplifying system with them. Xmas in central London appears to have got considerably worse in the time we have been away, but to say this would be to open myself up to the charge of having aged. So I try not to point out that even three years ago the natives weren't this drunk or aggressive. There was some part of Soho that hadn't yet been pissed on, and the blatantly fraudulent beggars were never in your face quite as much as this. But the crowds keep swarming here anyway, for whatever reason. Perhaps the fashion industry has managed to find a new way of making young women anorexic.

Perhaps drum 'n' bass got even louder. There is just so much talent in London. Everyone wants to be here, right now, where it's all happening.

Sasha draws a blank with the first few buskers, or beggars, as I like to call them. Then we station ourselves near Bar Italia, where a fat, gormless guitar-player is blundering through what might almost be a satirical deconstruction of 1950s jazz – hopelessly out of tune and out of time – except that he is entirely serious. Like the supposedly ironic deconstructionists, this guy couldn't do the real thing if he tried, but none of this swelling throng can tell the difference. He has thick unruly hair and enormous glasses with very thick lenses. His creased brown slacks and scuffed brown shoes would be appropriate on a much older person, but he's certainly not going to let that put him off. Some jazz musicians make the act of smoking look elegant and enviable. This guy has a fag jammed into the corner of his mouth, a full inch of ash hanging precariously off the end as he blinks myopically through the smoke. We have all come to the centre of the most fashionable city on earth and this is what we get – a duff busker yearning for the great days of swing.

'Let's ask him,' says Sasha, throwing ten pence into the guy's hat.

Just as I lean forward to tell her that this ham-fisted burk won't even know his own name, he answers in the affirmative. 'Yeah, I know Jamie.' Sasha gives me a dry smile. 'He sometimes plays in Covent Garden,' he says.

I busy myself seeing which cabaret acts are on at Ronnie Scott's. And wondering why people queue up to be insulted by their rude, stupid door staff. But when I've finished doing that I still have to look at Sasha's triumphant smile.

That's annoying, but not as irritating as the crowds of

tourists clustered around the buskers, all of whom are excruciating. Perhaps they see these street corner chancers as the free spirits they can no longer be, hampered as they are with jobs and families. Perhaps they are as tone-deaf as the buskers themselves. There must be some explanation.

Next up is a sax-player with scabs on his hollow chalk-white face. His act seems to consist of blurting and blathering all over a playalong jazz CD on a battered beatbox. Even his dog looks like it is on crack. He holds his sax above his head while twisting his body into contortions – all that stuff that pop video directors always ask for. I don't like to be judgemental, but he is clearly mentally and physically ill and obviously addicted to something. His crude, coarse tone is beneath contempt, but well above the threshold of pain. He has no sense of time, pitch or harmony, and yet he is honking along to Clifford Brown's 'Joyspring', an intricate piece of rapidly modulating bebop he has no hope of connecting with on any rational level. If the year were 1959 he would have had the excuse of being avant-garde. As it is, he succeeds only in being ignorant and infantile. The crowd love it. The nice people with the nice jobs and the nice children must think he represents everything they have left behind – poetry read by the light of the full moon, illicit sex, shoplifting to fill an empty belly, pawning the family jewels to buy shoes.

And everywhere we go the beggars keep asking for money from their floor-level pitches. Many of them now say thank you when you ignore them. The intention may be to try to head off any possible trouble, but it can sound sarcastic – at least it always does to my paranoid ears. A lad draped in a dirty blanket shoves a used McDonald's coffee cup in my face.

'Drop dead,' I tell him quietly. Fair comment, I would have thought.

'All right, mate, there's no need for that,' he says, swivelling to get a good look at me, rather surprised at this breach of correct etiquette. He carries on blocking the path, holding the cup up as if offering a refreshing drink to each passing tourist. He has dirty white skin and scabby dead eyes. Far from eliciting sympathy, this just serves to remind me that I can't afford to spend that much money on hard drugs. Why should I put my hand in my pocket to buy him more treats? Besides, as this is Old Compton Street he could have his choice of concerned older men who would take him away and feed and clothe him. They might require a few services in return, but I don't see why that should be a problem. Some people just don't want to work. They just want everything handed to them on a plate.

The heavy traffic and groups of slow-moving tourists on Charing Cross Road are almost a relief after Soho. Covent Garden piazza has a more-than-adequate sufficiency of street entertainment – human statues, buskers and barkers, the hustlers and the hopeless.

'So it's not the opera. Get over it,' says Sasha when I attempt to share my feelings.

'We might as well go home,' I tell her. 'We'll never find him. We're just wasting our . . .'

'It's him!' says Sasha, jumping up and down. 'It's Jamie!'

Jamie's demonic goatee, glittering eyes and kilt easily pick him out among the throng. He is rousing the rabble with some heavy metal accordion-playing, jigging around on heavy boots as he goes. After a while there is some tomfoolery with a penny whistle, a piercing folk tune that drives the mob into a frenzy. Soon they are clapping where they think the beat is, with generous allowance made for the many who are struggling to catch up. The effect could not have been any worse if they had offered a cash reward for deliberately trying to destroy the rhythm. Nevertheless, every single person present is having the time of their lives. Except me. Although we got there too late to hear him play the bagpipes so maybe the goddess has been smiling on us.

The crowd is loving the genuine carnival atmosphere – hellish noise, the stench of competing fast-food stalls, fake Gypsies slithering up to offer you lucky lavender. Lots of people will cherish this memory for the rest of their lives, but I will always remember the way Sasha's eyes are shining. When she looks at Jamie. Never mind that I intend to see Kate as soon as possible. It doesn't give Sasha the right to fall in love. Which is what this looks like. She joins in the thunderous applause at the climax to his act then joins in the orderly queue for CDs afterwards. As soon as he realises who it is, he yells her name. She reciprocates then throws her arms around him. As she only comes up to his chest, this means he has to bow his head to kiss her. I have ample opportunity to see just what a fine head of dark lustrous hair he has, not a hint of male pattern baldness in the offing. But I'll find something about him soon. Some chink in his armour. If they ever stop kissing.

'Hello!' I say, in Sasha's ear. 'Remember me?'

'Oh sorry. Jamie, this is Matt.'

Well, that's my real name gone. But presumably he knows her real one, and I don't know why we bother anyway. We *seem* to have got away with our crimes. Although you never know.

'Let's have a coffee!' says Jamie. 'I know just the place!'

It soon becomes clear that they intend to sit down in a place where poets and folk singers snipe at each other over brown rice. Wandering minstrels and scuffed troubadours are also encouraged to pick merry tunes on their guitars. After a short but wounding exchange it is agreed that I should be excused.

When the bright-eyed and perky Sasha returns to Stefan's it is with the grim news that this evening's fetish party has a school theme.

'Not old gits wandering around in school uniform,' I say.

'I like school stuff,' says Sasha, grinning and flashing her eyes. I never understood why she remains oddly enamoured of this quintessentially British kink.

'Most people into it are about ninety,' I tell her. 'Let's not exaggerate. They are often about seventy, that's seven, zero. Three score and ten. Just about dead.'

Sasha blows me a kiss.

'And then there are those spindly old geezers who hobble up in stockings and suspenders and point their bony fingers at you. It's like being marked for death. Their hands are so cold too.'

'You'll be old one day,' she says, and she is actually smiling fondly.

I should be pleased, I suppose. It makes a change from her telling me I am old already.

'And you have to have some old people with money anyway,' she says. 'They are the ones who pay for everything.'

It's true that many orgies barely cover costs because you always end up inviting people you like for free; the women hardly ever pay, and do we really want to be outnumbered by normal people? Those drunken football-loving morons whose idea of a great night out is no sex and a punch-up?

'They might well die on you. You do know that? These duff dads. These manky mentors. And what will Jamie say?'

She's smiling broadly now. I can't annoy her any more. Not with Jamie around. As a possible replacement.

'Where's the harm?' she says, smiling pityingly. 'Trying to make people happy? You should try it sometime. Aren't you dressing up?'

I shake my head. Boots and a leather thong seem so much more convenient, if you have the figure for it. And I do, my dears. I do.

'Doors shut at eleven,' says Sasha. 'We have to be there before then. What shall I wear?'

Stefan pretends to be interested in that, quisling that he is, while I play through one of Nigel Short's recent games on an onyx chess set. I have no idea of what's going on half the time, and I hate the oily bow-tied porker who annotated the game. But it beats playing 'Are my stocking seams straight?' with Sasha. She eventually appears in a school uniform and boater. It's cute, if too Benny Hill for my tastes. But it's still Her Supreme Loveliness. And that smile that can thaw the iciest of hearts.

'You really should have a costume,' she says to me. 'What about a bowler hat? And a suit? You'd look like Steed.'

Not the bloody Avengers again. As if it mattered what sort of supposedly stylish dross they used to put on black and white television in about 1960. I am looking at a woman who has been a professional dominatrix for many years. She was an enthusiastic amateur before that. She is even now, as a fugitive, a hard-core orgiast on the fetish scenes of more than one country. She is, in short (and quite short at five feet two inches), a bit of a goer. Someone you might fancy your chances with. Why would *she* get excited by some feeble references to kinky boots?

'It's stylish,' says Sasha as I cover my face with my trembling hands. 'And quirky.'

'Well, I love Diana Rigg,' I say.

'It's a long time since you've been that way about *me*!'

She put a lot of heft into that. And her eyes are burning. Have I neglected my duties as her personal therapist? Is there a contractual minimum of times you should say "I love you" to keep a long relationship going? 'If I didn't love you I wouldn't keep coming with you on all these mad adventures of yours,' I say. But she doesn't look happy. I should have just said 'I love you'. Why do we always have to keep on arguing all the time? Because we are partners, I suppose. There ain't no way round it.

'You don't "accompany me" anyway,' she says. 'You love stirring it up. You get a thrill from danger.'

'I do not.'

'You're much more of a psychopath than me . . . '

'Now look . . . '

'Look at Stefan,' she says, nodding over my shoulder where he has just entered.

I turn around expecting to see some pathetic overgrown schoolboy. Instead of which I'm looking at one of the most beautiful women I've ever seen. Long blonde hair, an enchanting smile, big blue eyes. He's all in black and it matches up – not just somewhere close, as I would have done. A cashmere polo neck over a mini-skirt, stockings and glossy knee-length boots. It's even the right clothes to trigger memories of my teenage years, when Julie Christie was a (mercifully) unobtainable goddess. For what on earth would we have done with her? Shown her our stamp collections? Stefan can see the effect she's having, acknowledging her devastating entrance with a brief *moue* of triumph.

'Hello,' he says, stressing the second syllable, then melts our hearts with another winsome smile. Laughter lines around his eyes crinkle. A flirtatious turn of the head to shield his laughing eyes and it's high time I stopped standing here like some love-struck old lecher. Even if that is precisely what I've just become. 'You must be Sasha's boyfriend. She's told me *such* a lot about you!'

Her voice is deeper than most women's, but it's higher than the real Stefan's. Thing is, this woman is so real she makes Stefan look like an awkward impostor in 'her' body.

'You look gorgeous . . . ' I say, rather flustered. 'What's your name?'

'Thank you,' he says, 'It's Stephanie.' He holds out a dainty hand which I kiss. His pink nail varnish is perfect. He gives me a knowing smile then hitches up his skirt to show a hint of white suspender belt – the little tart.

'I think you've pulled,' Sasha tells him. Or is it *her*?

'We must go,' says Stefan, looking at his watch. 'We cannot talk all night.'

'If you're going to be a woman, you're going to have to get used to being late,' I tell him, although I'm really talking to Sasha. Sasha says something that was quite uncalled for, then it's Stefan's turn to get on my tits.

'They close the doors at eleven!' he says. 'We must go! Immediately!'

'You're quite right, honey,' says Sasha, running her hands over his taut rump. 'The *customer* is always right.' She gives him an affectionate spank.

Stefan ignores this and flounces off, shiny heels clicking down the corridor.

'Hands off him; he's mine,' says Sasha, watching me watching him.

'Does that mean I'm stuck with Jamie?' I say.

'I don't fancy him . . .'

'Yeah, right . . .'

We bicker our way into the cab but then cheer up as I hand round some Es that Luke cabbed over – a free sample to help me make my mind up about buying in quantity.

The venue is a club in glamorous Bermondsey, where the old docklands are not quite gentrified yet but where there is ample space to play and the public will not be admitted. No humdrums clustered around the bar, no voyeurs getting in the way of sex play and no one walking between the floggers and the flogged. No loud music, no DJs, no gorillas on the door. Bliss. Especially so when the E starts to seep through our veins. The décor is 1970s glam – fluffy white rugs, glass-topped tables, enormous wicker thrones. There are some pro-doms present – which occasionally leads to tedious status games, as if it was a fantastic achievement to get men to humiliate themselves in pursuit of sex. But the down-market theme has kept the poseurs away. I can't say I'm comfortable in a room containing three men with full-length beards (one ginger), but the room is already reverberating to the sound of leather on flesh and it's only just opened.

Some of the men look like Tories – chinless wonders in dinner jackets and cummerbunds. It's almost as if they've stopped off on the way to the Last Night of the Proms. But let's face it, the Labour movement has nothing to boast about when it comes to the celebration of sexuality.

We find a couch and set about amassing sufficient supplies of carrots, celery and menthol gum to help the E course around our bodies. And to stop us yattering away like loons. Although it's already too late for that.

'Why don't you do "the Dance of Pan"?' says Sasha, knowing it will embarrass me.

'I only do it when I'm happy.' I'm talking through gritted teeth.

'Really?' asks Stefan, picking up on my embarrassment. '*Do* tell.'

'It's a sort of cancan,' says Sasha, while I put my hands over my face. 'He strips off and dances around with his hands behind his head. You really must see it.'

Thanks for sharing, dear. But as the E percolates through me I find myself stripped down to leather thong and boots. It's not quite optimum conditions for the Dance of Pan, but with Stefan and Sasha kissing and rubbing my body we are off to a good start.

Jamie struts in wearing a black rubber mini-skirt and top, his well-defined muscles slithering around under the tight latex. He joins us on our couch, where Sasha and I are fervently nibbling and nuzzling away. We have each other to chew on, and an admirer of Sasha has donated a Vicks inhaler, which may accentuate the buzz. It gives us something to do at least.

But does Sasha ever stop working? She has even managed to ask Jamie a question about the time he actually met the Dungeonmaster, in between saying 'Wow!' and 'Your eyes are really nice!' Jamie looks a little less invincible now.

'He's dangerous,' he says, looking at the floor.

H'm. Could the Dungeonmaster have bested him in combat? Or is he just wondering whether it's time to light up his hash-pipe again? Now that I can bear to look at him – this E really is good stuff – I can see that he has brown eyes: really bad news, according to the little prat whom the Dungeonmaster is promoting as a Black Metal superstar.

Perhaps that's what they argued about. Jamie's brown eyes just weren't Aryan enough. But how would a veggie animal rights activist come into contact with the Dungeonmaster anyway? I can't ask him because Sasha is rubbing her leg against his and staring into his eyes.

'Do you think he has genuine occult power?' she asks.

For some reason Jamie considers this seriously. 'He definitely knows the sleight of hand stage magic that looks like real magic if you don't know any better. What Uri Geller does.'

'Can *you* do all that?' says Sasha. Her eyes are shining. She is doing everything apart from wagging her tail.

'No,' says Jamie. His eyes briefly collide with mine, as he checks to see how Sasha's escort for the night is taking this, the guy he will soon have to edge out of position. 'Can't do conjuring tricks,' he continues, shrugging to indicate that he could if he wanted to. 'Can't do serious karate. Can't do the yoga that Tibetan bods do – hypnosis, ESP, astral travel and so forth. He can. Or could back then. He's a hard nut. But twisted. He's bisexual.'

'So are most people we know,' Sasha says.

'Yeah. But it's not easy for someone in his position. *You* don't have to command an army of homophobic Nazis.'

'Don't put ideas into her head,' I say.

'Yeah,' says Sasha. 'What would I *ever* do if someone did what *I* want for a change?' There is a pause during which Jamie wisely decides not to say anything.

'How come you know all this stuff?' I ask him.

He stares off into the distance for a while.

'A girl I knew got involved with them. She eventually committed suicide. I don't really want to talk about it until I've finally *done* something about it.'

Sasha looks at me as if to say, 'Why aren't you like this?' I raise a languid eyebrow at her. Then I pop another E. This *does* feel nice.

'What's that accent of yours?' I ask him, an annoying habit of mine. I would have a fit if anyone claimed I was a Liverpudlian. Even though I am.

'Scottish,' he says, still looking at Sasha.

'It's very light,' I say. 'I never knew you were Scottish.'

'I was born in Scotland but, as Wellington said, just because I was born in a stable it does not make me a horse.'

Sasha thinks that's a lot funnier than it actually is. I remember when she used to smile like that at me. When we first met. Well, Jamie. You might actually be tough enough to handle her. And at least you've got the weapons to defend yourself with. You'll need them.

While they chatter I spot two guys having a mock-heroic fencing match with their canes, bantering away merrily as they cross swords. I really wish I hadn't seen that. Good clean fun tends to get on my nerves. And here's more of it. Someone has decided to have a caning competition, a test of endurance for the submissives and a posing contest for the dominants. I'm paraphrasing here. The tops see it as a chance to be seen as the most powerful, mighty and skilful dominant ever, or at least the best one at an orgy in in south-east London on an ice-cold December evening. While three submissives have decided to show the rest of us the real meaning of stoicism. They will compete to take the longest and hardest beating ever dished out. Organising this seems to involve a great deal of rivalry and internecine bitching, a squabble that eventually becomes almost as bitter as deciding the order of acts at a pub poetry reading. Except that tonight there actually are some people in the audience. And someone might remember who won.

Jamie is warming his slave up frantically, veins bulging all over his arms as he quickly brings an all-over glow to the proffered buttocks. Without this preliminary, blood might be spilled, which means instant disqualification. His competitors are playing it cooler, but it is clear that everyone wants to win.

The woman with the microphone has soft lovely eyes, ruby-red lips and auburn hair leaking out from a black leather cowboy hat. Her shiny lizardskin suit is tucked into knee-length boots. She has playing cards, dollar signs and dice painted on her fingernails. 'Vegas Nails!' whispers Stefan. Some might consider a pint of ale and a fag not the ideal accoutrements for one with such lovely curves, but some would certainly not say that to her face. She has presence. And a number of men crawling around after her wherever she goes. She certainly knows how to use her voice to shut everyone up. First we get The Rules, of which there are far too many. But then I always say that, whatever game we are playing. To cut Madame Z's speech short, apart from saying that drawing blood disqualifies both partners, she announces: 'Some subs have complained about being caned by a man. This is regrettable. Men should not be concerned about being punished by other men. We are here to celebrate sexual diversity.' It's a valid point. Although somewhat undermined by what Jamie says to his slave. 'So bend over, you big poof.' The slave's laughter is a trifle forced.

The caning commences. Very soon it becomes clear that none of the subs is going to drop out. Civilisations could wax and wane, the sun could flicker and die out – perhaps Cliff Richard might even stop releasing pop records. But we would still be here, watching three doms scouring these glowing red bottoms. It's not just the E making me impatient; twenty minutes later there is still no sign of anyone dropping out. Eventually, Madame Z is forced to invent a number of spurious pretexts to disqualify people: talking, smiling, the moon is in Pisces. And two winners are declared. Mistress Sarah has proved once more that her Scorpionic energy often leaves her grateful slaves with a sting in the tail. And the winning sub is a bloke I still don't know after ten years of seeing him grovel. Barely has the applause died down before he is looking for someone to give him a proper caning – his bottom still isn't quite as leathery as the average rhinoceros hide. Jamie takes his unfair disqualification like a gentleman, which is more than I would have done, and we are pounced on by a women called Penny.

I've played with everyone at the party,' she tells Jamie and me. She is fresh and vital, and practically naked. Her eyes are swimming with something or other; certainly alcohol is present in the mix. The hash-pipe is produced. Jamie tells us what a swiz it was being disqualified from the competition, without being bitter as I would have been, and then Penny wants us to accompany her to the Ladies.

'Most certainly, my dear,' says Jamie.

I smile weakly, but there's no point in trying to freeze Jamie out any longer. He's coming on Sasha's expedition; we will have to get along. But I can't cope with this many strangers in this quick succession. This probably won't work. But something is telling me that I have to squeeze into a cubicle in the Ladies. Just because I've never done it before.

Unfortunately, this doesn't seem a valid reason according to my genitals.

Underneath my leather thong it feels like a Siberian winter.

But the situation is intriguing none the less. Intriguing? I wouldn't be anywhere else than here. She is shaved except for about a small cluster of delicate hairs above the cleft. Her skin is very white and smooth, not a hint of the shaving rash that can afflict those who neglect to use moisturiser. Penny rips my thong off, something I hadn't expected and am not that thrilled about. Jamie is fully erect, hot to trot. I am fully not erect. And this is the sort of situation where inappropriate comparisons may be made. While buttoning up my thong I have ample time to wonder why I don't fancy her. She's beautiful, young and bright – if skewed on some combination of mind-altering substances, mostly booze. But whatever Sasha and Kate have isn't present. They are both looking at me. Some statement is required from me before anything else can happen.

'Sorry, I've got too much emotional baggage at the moment,' I say, feeling rather foolish. Not a ripple of comprehension disturbs her lovely face. And in any case, she couldn't care less. It couldn't be less relevant. She clambers on to the cistern and instructs me to sit on the seat.

'I'm going to piss all over you,' she says, trying on a bossy voice that doesn't quite fit. But it's delightful hearing her try it. To encourage more of this I sit down facing her. Suddenly her hand is clamping my head to her pussy. Her grip is way too hard. 'The only perversion is coercion' springs to mind. Unfortunately, I am presently unable to convey this to my playmate because I have a mouth full of squishy vaginal lips, all the more delicious for the lack of hair. It's heaven breathing her in, waiting for her warm flow. In fact, as this moment actually exists it's considerably better than a slice of pie-in-the-sky.

She gasps as she finally plucks up courage to do it. Her

flow is delicate, mildly tangy, pleasantly insouciant. It's hard keeping up with the gushing fluid, but I just about manage it. Unfortunately, she wants to play mistress and slave. As if I don't have enough of that at home. 'Lick the piss out of there,' she says, all cold and autocratic again – at least, that was the intention. She's far too sweet and lovely for that tone of voice. The contradiction between intention and result triggers a great swell of warm-hearted affection inside me. I suppose Sasha would say it was *cute*. And I suppose the great majority of the public would be running back to their gardening programmes on the telly at this point. But that's their loss.

'Can we lose the role-play?' I ask her in a gentle, hopefully non-confrontational way. She looks down, mildly amused under the thrilled swimming eyes. 'I don't mind worshipping your magnificence,' I say, entirely truthfully. 'Just don't tell me to do it.'

There is a cliffhanging pause where we all think about how revealing that was. Although it's just possible that Jamie is more concerned about getting his dick polished and Penny would prefer to use my mouth for something far more useful than unloading psychological trivia. As they're right and I'm wrong I kneel on the floor and set to kissing her. It seems to me that she needs a lot of work on the lower curves of her bum, her damp cleft and all the other nooks and crannies I can find. Somewhere up there a more primal exchange is taking place, but I worship in my own way, although all too conscious that Sasha may enter the Ladies at any point and see my red boots sticking out of the toilet stall. After that we take it in turns to gently spank her and whisper encouragement in her ear while she squirms her way through what may be several orgasms. There is certainly plenty of moaning and groaning going on, but what it signifies is presently a secret between Penny and whatever Goddess she is praying to. Sometime later she comes back to the material plane. As if far less had happened, she suddenly stands up, adjusts what little clothes she is wearing and beams at us both.

'You boys!' she says, all flirtatious, then trips out of the toilet, walking on air.

Jamie and I look at each other, a teeny-weeny bit embarrassed. Young Americans may have swapped high fives at this point, but we are still avoiding each other's eyes. Is that sort of thing really 'on'? How should the genteel poor behave just after three-way fetish sex? Should two gentlemen be stood in a toilet cubicle together, now Penny's gone? No. They shouldn't, actually. That's easy enough to agree on.

As we emerge for a wash and brush up, the door opens to admit a number of giggling women. Riding the rush from the last fifteen minutes even I can banter my way through that one.

Then we find Sasha back on our couch where she asks us what we have been up to. It's a good question. One that has to be answered in a way that doesn't make her feel insecure. And that is the way of Lao-tzu. The way that is no way. It just doesn't exist. A pre-emptive strike is probably the safest option.

'I need your wee,' I tell her, holding out a glass. Her eyes pop a little. But then her smile spreads. She's flattered. Even better, Jamie seems a bit squeamish about this perfectly harmless hobby of mine. 'I want to see if we can recycle the E,' I tell him as he does his best not to show his revulsion. 'You can charge yourself up again from wee.'

'Don't like chemicals,' says Jamie. 'Stick to the herb.'

Well, that's all well and good, but I can't take the paranoia any more.

'Go on, babe,' I say, giving her my pint glass. 'Fill her up.'

Sasha excuses herself. Jamie fills in the time until her return with a monologue which is understandably euphoric, given our recent activities. Sasha's eyes are sparkling as she returns with a clear glass of lightly fragrant fluid.

'That's so lovely,' I tell her. 'It's almost like having your pussy in a glass.'

She's giggling now, although Jamie doesn't look very well.

'And it tastes of E! Maybe it's going to work one more time!'

That horrible chemical taste is indeed there. One more reason to gulp this liquid down.

'Sasha says you are a musician,' says Jamie, handing me a lit hash-pipe.

'Not any more,' I tell him, when I've finished coughing and retching. Some of the smoke stays down though.

'What did you play?'

'Jazz.'

'Oh.' He doesn't need to say any more. A pall of gloom briefly descends. Then Jamie tells me a lot about the history and current state of morris dancing, in particular the fiercely competitive alternative variety. It would seem that even fetish morris dancing still makes more sense to most people than a fiercely algebraic music like jazz. Something which requires more thought than just getting pissed and hitting each other with sticks.

'You should try it,' says Jamie, absolutely seriously. 'Get out in the fresh air and have some fun.'

I can't help laughing as the bliss chemicals continue to

divide and multiply, having their own little orgy inside my veins.

'Never understood jazz fans,' he says. 'Miserable bunch.'

He does have a point. Jazz fans do like their sad stories about American outcasts, preferably dead ones. They're looking for elegant sepia-tinted misery, which must be safely in the past. Today's tragedies interest them not in the least. The musicians are not much better, always moaning on interminably. Many of them set out to confound the expectations of the listeners and then spend the rest of their lives complaining there is no audience.

'I suppose I set out to fail,' I tell him, although he can hardly have any idea of what I'm talking about.

'So you've succeeded then,' he says, too jovially for my taste.

Before that winds me up too much, Stefan arrives and prostrates himself before us, flipping up his skirt to offer us a brief tantalising glimpse of his oiled and reddened bum. Sasha applies some gentle pressure on his shoulders and he is soon on all fours, his proffered rump offering all sorts of delights – chief among which is a way out of this conversation with Jamie. I was once patronised by an actress who hadn't worked for twenty years – but she was still a thespian, and therefore a cut above the rest of us. And now I've got tin whistle-playing morris dancers having a go.

Stefan moans lightly as Sasha strokes his bottom. She squirts lube from her ever-ready supply then rubs it in where it will do most good. The flesh altar is prepared. All sorts of sacraments may now be celebrated. Sasha gives my pouch a squeeze. Her eyes twinkle. 'You're loving this, aren't you? And when the E wears off . . . '

Which it hasn't just yet, but there's still people to meet,

flashing lights to dance inside my eyelids and a gently euphoric wave to ride. It's midnight. When young men kill each other in kebab shops. When blood splatters on to the pavements outside pubs. All over the world drunken hooligans are looking for people to beat up. Tomorrow's papers have just hit the streets, giving decent people another chance to fulminate against the outsiders in our midst. But it seems quite nice here, with the sex and drug addicts – the real threat to our society.

Sasha has bought a toy from one of the stalls, a springy black prong which would fit snugly up anyone's fundament.

'I bought this for you,' says Sasha. She knows she's being a little bit naughty presenting this in front of Jamie. Even sex-positive men can be a bit funny about the sight of a bulbous black butt-plug thrust into general view. It's not the sort of thing you want to see when chaps get together. The implement wobbles lewdly on Sasha's upturned palm.

'Heigh-ho,' says Jamie, leaping to his feet. 'Must find someone to flog. Bye-ee.' He strides off, swishing his crop.

'This reminds me of Nails,' I say, just to watch her recoil in horror. Nails was a black drug dealer who was murdered in our New York apartment a few years back. His dick was severed in the process. You can't joke about it. Although the left side of Sasha's mouth has twitched upwards.

'We never did that ritual to reform Osiris,' she says.

'What?'

'You know the old myth. Osiris was castrated. Like Nails was. If his body is not re-formed there will be eternal chaos on earth.'

'So *that's* what happened.'

'Where did his dick end up anyway? I thought you had it.'

'No! You had it. In that bottle of chilli vodka . . . '

She smiles. Listen to us. Bickering away. She reaches into her bag and rolls a fresh black condom over the pear-shaped plug.

'You could make it all right again,' she says. 'It's a pretty tenuous connection. But I could certainly place this implement somewhere it would do Stefan the world of good. And me. And Sasha.

'So there will be peace on earth,' I say. '*If* we plant this sacred lance . . . er, in the moist earth of Germany?'

Sasha picks it up and runs with it.

'You'd also be fucking a Nazi – sorry, Stefan, nationalist – with a black man's dick.'

'I'm not even a nationalist,' comes the muffled protest until Sasha silences him with a swipe of her crop.

'Probably not the first time that's happened.'

'In Bermondsey?'

'Especially in Bermondsey. What about the docks?'

Stefan is pawing at our feet now, pleading for ingress.

'Heal the rift,' whispers Sasha. 'Make it right for Nails. For Osiris. For you. For me . . .'

I gently ease the plug in as Stefan lets out a deep sigh of satisfaction.

Sasha strokes his back and whispers encouragement in his ear. She hugs me tightly. Her eyes have mooned out into great soft beds of sweet devotion. Love, soft sweet love, bathes us endlessly. It's the end of the rainbow, the first day of the summer holidays, Xmas at five years old. But better than a dream or a memory. We're here now, in the moment. And the knowledge that three days ago I was suspended in frozen animation in Bavaria makes me laugh out loud. Until Sasha starts to look a bit concerned.

Sometime later, after a bit of a wallow in what my old

Buddhist guru used to call 'the mire of sensuality', I'm telling
Sasha we have found peace on earth. Just in time for Xmas.
But the warriors disagree. Jamie is negotiating terms.

'So you come to Germany with us,' says Sasha. She men-
tions a large sum of money. Several thousand pounds. Just for
risking his life for a week or so. It's high time *my* allowance
was increased actually, but Sasha is staring intently at Jamie.
There seems to be some tension as to whether he will accept
her gracious offer. Until he takes her hand and kisses it, a
little too fervently for my liking.

'My sword is at your command, madam. I am ready to
serve.'

'I'll bet you are, mate,' I tell him. He looks at me as if I
have somehow ruined a great solemn moment. Maybe I have.
But I want him to know that I'm on a mission too. And that
is a quest to hold on to Sasha.

'We have found the first of our knights!' says Sasha,
hugging me tighter. And it would be churlish to step on her
good mood. She is so happy right now. And the next five
minutes of hugging and kissing would seem to reaffirm love.
We are so in love. After seven years. This is the happy ending.
If only we stopped now.

7

The thirteen months of the menstrual calendar also led to pagan reverence for the number 13, and Christian detestation of it. Witches' 'covens' were supposed to be groups of 13 like the moon-worshipping dancers of the Moorish zabat (sabbat) to whom thirteen expressed the three-in-one nature of the lunar goddess.

The Women's Encyclopedia of Myths and Secrets
by Barbara G. Walker

SASHA DEVELOPED A TASTE for driving around in an old taxi last time we lived in London. And rather than hire a car for a few weeks she has bought another one. From the man who used to do our repairs. This is hardly living undercover, I would have thought, but she is confident that the police are too busy to bother about people we have inadvertently killed. We're also too busy to worry about it. Sasha has arranged plenty of other dangerous and frightening things for us to do. The first ordeal is driving around central London and finding a parking place. In the Xmas rush. While the streets have been ripped apart. As we sit seething and swearing it is not much consolation to know that this is so that other people can make a fortune on the Internet. For some of this time I comfort myself by patting my jacket where I have stored the black butt-plug, still sheathed in the condom that nestled inside Stefan, sealed inside a white rubber glove. It's relatively fresh, because Stefan used an enema before his night out – the little poppet – but a hint of spice remains to liven up the desperately slow and noisy journey into town. I don't like to use words like fetishism – needlessly pathological names coined by killjoys in white coats. But I do want to hang on to this souvenir of a memorable evening. And Sasha thinks that preserving our work from last night for as long as possible will aid our mission. Listen to me. *Her* mission.

Once we have finally arrived I have to pretend to be one of the Dungeonmaster's minions to pick up his English mail. Just as Sasha said, they didn't even ask for proof of identity. They just handed over a big wedge of mail destined for the English branch of the Odin's Knot Society. As I sign for the post I notice my handwriting is strikingly similar to my father's. I feel the usual stab of pain that he is no longer with us, although ameliorated by the knowledge that there is one less reason to pretend to be respectable now. I wonder how Sasha is going to cope with her mother's death. But perhaps this manic activity is the best way of coping. There's certainly no sign of her slowing down as she grabs the mail off me and starts to rip it open in the street.

Round the corner from the postbox service is a family-run Italian café. Sasha and I are in agreement that we shouldn't really drink another coffee today, specifically I should not be on my fifth big mug of grump juice. Before lunch. But addicts need to lose the battle occasionally. It might as well be against caffeine as all the other things we must never have. At least coffee only causes pointless bickering, paranoid rages and inappropriate use of physical violence on domestic appliances.

The liquid slops over my hands as I make my way to our table, reminding me of Sasha's theory that heavy caffeine-users experience motor dysfunction. A further manifestation of my condition appears as I attempt to put sugar in Sasha's coffee, showering us with granules.

'The Dark Lord defeated by a sugar sachet,' says Sasha in an unnecessarily cutting tone.

'You shouldn't use that stuff anyway . . . ' I tell her in a pathetic attempt at retrieving face.

'I know,' said Sasha. 'It makes my piss taste sweet.'

While this is true I hadn't necessarily wanted to share it with the man next to us. His face freezes with revulsion and terror as he starts to brush himself off with a vehemence more appropriate to peeling off child beggars. When he has finished his big production number he bristles off to another table. He props up his *Evening Standard* with much froth and bluster and resumes reading that simpering ninny Brian Sewell.

'It's amazing how guys like Brian Sewell can get so worked up all the time . . . ' I say.

'Yes,' butts in Sasha. 'It's almost as if some people get off on righteous indignation. And ranting on and on all day.'

I drink some more coffee rather than refute this. There's no need to descend to her level. Not that that's particularly easy, what with her being a dwarf. She's actually a little bit taller today, having just bought some silly shoes by Jean-Paul Gaultier. These green tartan wedges look nice but don't seem much use for walking around in, if you don't mind me being all masculine about it. I nod my way through Sasha's description of her muscle cramps, planning what might happen after

I have massaged her knotted calves. There are still *some* things I might be required for. She rips some envelopes open.

'Listen to this! "I enclose a donation for your important work." A thousand pounds!'

She rips the cheque up then does a seated cheerleader's dance. She wants to show me that we have in fact achieved something. And that I am wrong. Again.

'You were right,' I tell her. 'I was wrong. I'm sorry.'

There is a long silence while she stares at me suspiciously. I don't crack, though, and the apology is finally accepted at face value. More fool her.

'We might get some clues as to where the winter sacrifice will be,' says Sasha, ripping open more envelopes. 'Where he *really* lives these days.'

One of the correspondents has inked in the Odin's Knot symbol at the end of his letter. I remember the same sort of desire to join someone or something. When I was about twelve.

'Perhaps I should get their symbol tattooed on me,' I tell her. 'That noose thing. It will make us look more convincing.'

'Yeah!' She nods briskly, happy I'm getting with the programme but still too busy actually to look at me. 'I'm starting to think that the legend of Odin hanging upside down is the source of the original Tarot image,' she says, dividing the violated mail into a pile of envelopes and correspondence.

'The hanged man?' I say. 'Could be. Might as well add another level of mystery to it. Something else we'll never know the answer to. Did you find the address yet?' I ask her.

'No, but there's some good leads to follow up here. I can trace this lot on Stefan's computer.'

This sounds like a good moment to leave her to it. She

works so much better on her own, as she herself has often told me.

To get the tattoo I visit an old-school tattooist near King's Cross, the sort of place that does swastikas or even football colours. I'm not particularly fastidious, but the reception area would make a mortician gag. The carpet is scrofulous and stinking. As are the other men waiting, occupied by nothing other than projecting dumb malevolence. They will never be able to say what circumstances produced this near-catatonic state – thankfully. I don't want to hear about it and neither does anyone else. Some people think I look frightening, but they haven't a clue. These battered faces are brick-red or fungus-white, thin and ratty or fat and porcine. Their blood-shot eyes are presently on standby, perhaps permanently, or maybe until another input of lager or sport will spark them back into life again. There is a bit of a wait before I can be tattooed, but it's not the sort of place you want to sit in reading a book. You should really be gnawing on a bone, or scraping the dried blood off your new trainers. I try looking at my Psion for a while, as Sasha has downloaded Milton's *Paradise Lost* from a Satanic website. She thought I should check out the portrayal of Satan as a glamorous rebel and God as a bumbling duffer. Unfortunately, I don't get very far before a message from God himself appears – in the shape of Bill Gates's Microsoft system: 'Too many spelling errors in John Milton, *Paradise Lost*, to keep displaying them.' Well, that's all we need to know about some limey called John Milton. I press PLAY on my mini-disk. Stefan has recorded some ancient Icelandic chants for me to learn, part of the Dungeonmaster's minimal entrance requirements.

I have very few days left to start learning these bone-freezing yodels, but it's not exactly easy listening. Apologists for the warriors' creed of Odinism sometimes say that these ideas and symbols were misused by the Nazis. But would an eleventh-century runic visionary really have been that worried by a spot of genocide a thousand years on? It seems doubtful that he or she would have wanted their descendants to sit round listening to whalesong and sending their money to buy African dictators more guns – sorry, make that 'feed the starving'. What is certain is that the ancient art of chanting rune songs letter by letter, syllable by syllable, can sound rather silly on occasion. Particularly when the artiste is a Texan man singing in what he thinks is Old Norse. It's particularly unfortunate when it comes to 'Os', the rune that signifies the primal breath, the word 'knowledge' and the All-Father Odin. It just sounds remarkably like a man chanting the word 'arse' over and over again. Zipping through the tracks just gets me more epic poetry in English and ancient Norwegian. As if I didn't already know that life was cold and hard long ago. Not that it will be any easier this time next week, unless I manage to brainwash my own little ice warrior.

I call Luke to see if the Ecstasy has arrived. Once that has been confirmed I don't even mind having my skin ripped apart with a motorised needle-gun. I have often been tattooed by wild-eyed visionaries who saw themselves as shamans. They wanted to invoke mystic forces by carving gods and demons into my flesh. This guy is a butcher in a bloodstained T-shirt. I picture Jamie as the pain sears through me. It's exactly the moment to send a curse. 'Hands off her, or I'll have you, mate,' seems appropriate, especially in these sur-roundings. As the sharp pain intensifies I can see a bearded ancestor of mine materialising out of a red mist, broadsword at the ready. New Agers and bogus fortune-tellers will always tell you to get in touch with a Native American spirit healer. But don't be surprised if the line is permanently engaged. Or the service provider has some difficulty in hooking you up. It's always better to work with the local Godforms, at least if you want results.

Picking up the Ecstasy involves meeting another middle-youth hooligan, a drummer whose drug-use has transformed his face into a big slice of veal with two dabs of cranberry sauce for eyes. His grin is sincere but sets off a ripple of flabby new chins and an off-white glimmer of chipped teeth. It's too frightening to return. Until I catch my own reflection in the wing mirror and decide that guys like us might as well stick together. Luke's business is presently conducted from his motor, also his place of residence whenever his wife has decided that his cocaine dealing is affecting his parenting skills. He spends a lot of time in the car. And there is only so much that little stick-on pine tree air fresheners can do. We are now parked at the Shoreditch end of the Hackney Road, within sight of three different lap-dancing bars. Two of them have grim apes in dinner jackets stood by red velvet ropes on brass stanchions.

'Nice to see this area coming up in the world,' I say, nodding at a dead rat on the pavement.

'I like the East End,' says Luke, chewing on his ever-present gum. If he didn't have the gum his chemical consumption would have him chewing his lips off. 'You get the best prices for everything. I've got some really good coke!'

'Really? Hunt the coke in among the speed and aspirin?'

'Nah, that's all changed, mate. This stuff's pukka.'

Course it is. I give him a roll of notes and he gives me

fifty tabs of Ecstasy. Which is nearly enough to get Sasha to calm down for ten minutes or so. Perhaps I could crush it up and mix it in with whatever swill the Dungeonmaster's army lives on. If Sasha manages to find the address in among all that stolen correspondence.

'You've got the *Illuminatus* trilogy!' I say, picking up a thick paperback from the floor. This occult conspiracy epic seemed very good when I was living on beer, magic mushrooms and grass. It would probably be foolish to go back to it though. Now I'm all grown up. 'How far have you got?' I ask him.

'It's my son's. He's turning into a right little hippie,' he says.

'You'd like it,' I tell him. He picks it up, cracks it open and reads a few sentences at random, before tossing the wearisome, all-too-heavy item back on the shelf.

'Got no time for reading,' he says.

I have heard this a lot recently, quite often from people with degrees, and once from a woman with a degree in English Literature. We could after all be sat in a traffic jam talking on a mobile phone on our way to buy a computer that will be obsolete by the time we get home. We could then play with shaky digital pictures of ourselves or scroll through acres of ill-informed speculation or endure endless marketing scams. We could send this swill to our friends by e-mail, if our gear's working, if the manufacturers bothered to test it before putting it on sale. That would certainly be an improvement on frittering away £7.99 on anything with words in it. Read a book? When you can look at pictures? Are you thick, mate?

But a distaste for print may be a side-effect of Luke having all these chemical love pills to play with. By the time I have had a few more Es even I may be reading less and dancing a little bit more. Although I will be happy if it just de-programmes Sasha. I'm sick of this Warrior Queen stuff. I want her all fluffy again.

'I don't want any more E!' says Sasha, back at Stefan's. By the look on her face you would think I had offered her a lifetime's subscription to the *Reader's Digest*. 'But I'm nearly out of Prozac,' she says.

'It's time you packed that stuff in. It doesn't work anyway.'

'You just don't *want* me to get better.'

'Are you hungry? Shall I get you a yoghurt from the fridge?'

'Get me some Prozac! It keeps me positive! Get me some. Go on!'

So that's another humiliating errand I will have to go on – telling a quack I'm depressed to get legal drugs. Did Peter Ustinov really once say that the drug culture was a 'fancied flight on borrowed wings'? Well, he may have done, sometime in my troubled adolescence – if he hadn't been too busy going back to the buffet for another ten portions of trifle. Obviously, it's much better to trough out until you look like a hippo with a serious impulse control problem. Then you really should grow a small thin beard to mask how fat you are. That always works.

And why shouldn't my little light-bringer have some chemical help? She is in a bad way presently. Her mom dying is really getting to her. All of a sudden she loves her. But she can't be there to tell her. Plus there is the delayed reaction from a few murders, and she was quite possibly mad before all that started. Basically, if she wants Prozac she shall have it. Even if it seems a little inappropriate to send a man with a shiny new warrior tattoo on such an errand.

'I *could* see if Dr Chang is still dishing it out,' I tell her, my heart sinking at the thought of a trip back to the bleakest part of the Elephant and Castle. She nods, neither approving nor disapproving. We both know that running around in the fresh air would probably combat depression much quicker. But we file that with other truthful little nuggets like: 'We are all going to die.' It's true, but not helpful.

The next day there is a long wait at our old Doctor's, which I fill by tensely flicking through old copies of *Vogue* – the perfect choice for a waiting room of street alkies and zonked mothers weighed down by lively children. By the time I finish reading *Vogue* I am all too aware that a great many people earn more money than me and that even more have inherited stupefying quantities of cash. Many useless products and services have been invented and we must buy them – immediately if not sooner. And as it's a quarter of a century since my brief attempt at being a student, I should probably stop talking like one. I am here to make Sasha 'happy' – the real Holy Grail, which she has recently confused with chasing after the Dungeonmaster.

But Dr Chang does not look happy. Something is up. And it's more than a hangover or family problems. Whatever it is, I can tell he is going to be a hard sell. I stumble and mumble my way through a brief explanation of my predicament. A few sentences about depression, long history of, trouble sleeping, and so on, should be enough to get me some Prozac.

'Have you ever considered counselling?' he says, seriously as far as I can make out.

I sit up and stare straight into the man's eyes, attempting to fix him to his wall calendar (which has been supplied by the manufacturers of the very drug I need). 'I have had five different types of therapy,' I begin, and then, seeing that I had unintentionally frightened him, lower my voice, 'and the last time was with an addiction counsellor in his twenties who had never been addicted to anything. He kept referring to me in the third person: "And what does Matt think about that?" '

I've said my real name instead of the fake one I am presently trading under, but he's not that bothered. Or that interested in the rest of it. He is not nodding or empathising in any way. Maybe he just doesn't like me. It does happen.

'Are you married?' he asks.

I tell him I live alone. Don't laugh, but it's theoretically sadder to be single for some reason. He nods sagely. Everyone knows that married men are less miserable than bachelors. I don't tell him about the recent survey which insists that married women are less happy than single girls – many of whom spend their entire existence complaining that they want to be married. Maybe we all know too much to be happy now. How on earth did they manage it in the 1950s? Perhaps it was the light music they used to listen to. Maybe that cheery tuneful stuff actually lifted the spirits. Just give me the happy pill, I feel like telling him. Then you can see someone you might be able to cure and I can go home and put some Miles Davis on. At least he knew how to make a living out of misery and madness. Though it may have helped having rich parents and a pretty face.

Dr Chang still hasn't reached for the prescription pad, so I tell him I am suicidal. And I have already tried every type of therapy and counselling ever invented – which is almost true. I stopped bothering with the talking cures shortly after the first killing. You can't talk *that* over with a therapist. Not really.

'I just feel another type of Prozac with fewer side-effects might work for me,' I say.

'They all have side-effects,' he says.

It's odd how they didn't mention that in the non-stop media barrage of approval for Prozac a few years back. Anyone would think that giant pharmaceutical companies can just foist any old rubbish on the media and journalists will just lap it up. Permanent happiness in a pill. It's just *got* to work, hasn't it? Dr Chang eventually gives in and I get back home with my stash, wondering why on earth anyone would bother painting the Elephant and Castle shopping centre mauve. It was bad enough when it was pink. The first thing Sasha wants to know on my return is if she can take two of them to kick-start it.

'Why not?' I tell her. 'It's more of an instant lift.'

She narrows her eyes.

'You're looking perky,' she says. 'Have you had any?'

'No. Well. Just half an E. I'm a bit whacked after the other night. I'll have a few of these too. It's meant to help prolong the buzz.'

Soon I am feeling as sick as the last time I tried this stuff. The side-effects include digestive upheavals, nausea, insomnia and manic aggression when the supply is cut off. As I said, they don't have the same sort of publicity budget for that little lot. But forty-five minutes later the sun comes up. Whoosh. It suddenly feels like we are supposed to be here. For once. Maybe normal people feel like this all the time. Pleasure – that's the word I was looking for. And why not ring Kate's London number? What harm could it do?

'I fancy seeing Luke again tonight,' I tell Sasha, trying to clear a space to see Kate.

'We are going to the theatre,' she says very firmly. '*Antony and Cleopatra.*'

'Oh *that*? Helen Mirren in the nude?'

'Well, that would be *really* radical,' says Sasha, who hates most actresses.

There was a pause while I decided not to say anything about the cutting, caustic tone of voice she employed for that one. It might well have been unfair that Sasha herself was not allowed to be in some terrible short films once upon a time. But it's also just possible that Helen Mirren might be better at real acting.

'Alan Rickman's in it,' she says, nodding approvingly.

'He must be really handsome if you don't mind his beard,' I say. 'I mean, what if I grew a beard? What then?'

'It would be distinguished. Flecked with grey. A salt-and-pepper beard.'

'The choice of winos the whole world over. And jazz musicians, of course. I suppose it helps the inevitable transition from one to the other.'

'I like beards.'

'Because of your dad?'

'You're much better than him.'

Does she mean it? How will I ever know?

'Your dad really was tough. He could kill a man with his bare hands.'

'You did that,' she says, coming up to me and starting to stroke my leg.

'Yes, but he could do it on purpose. While sober,' I tell her, 'and in a real war. More than once. I killed a man with a weak neck. Who was drunk.'

'It was still a great punch! And what about the other guy . . . ?'

'Never mind about that . . .'

Sasha's eyes are shining. She is purring at me. She is probably exuding 'fuck me' pheromones. Killers are just *so* hot. Needless to say I don't feel like it right now. I'll fancy it later. When Sasha doesn't.

'What if I compared you with my mother all the time?' I ask.

'I'm nothing like her!' she says, although she has no idea of what the other bane of my life looks like.

Now I come to think of it, they are both bossy little things. There might even be a slight resemblance between the two of them. My sister's short too. I feel a bit queasy now. Change the subject. 'So you won't run off with Jamie just yet?' I ask, hoping to catch her off-guard.

'No way! You'd just turn me in. So we're stuck.'

'Perhaps all married couples should murder a couple of people after a few years or so,' I say. 'Just to bond together. Like we did. It's so much better than counselling.'

'Maybe they should murder the counsellors,' she says.

'Now you're talking.'

We share a fond smile and a warm glow. Some of this is Ecstasy and Prozac and some of it is seven years of love. But just then she asks me what she will wear. And darkness descends until we are finally ready to leave.

London train journeys used to be enlivened by red-faced men in white shirts saying 'I'm on the train' into their mobile phones. Now it's the entire population of south London telling each other 'I'm on the bus'. As ever, the stupider the person, the louder the voice. We should have walked but Sasha doesn't mind, having decided to double her Prozac dose for the foreseeable future. We are in better luck with the beggars along the bleak wasteland of the South Bank. No one wants our money and, joy of joys, there are no buskers. No one frazzles our nerves with a travesty of 'music, that moody food of us that trade in love', as Cleopatra says. And why do these supposedly poor people use amplifiers? Why? And aren't the police meant to persecute wandering vagrants and threatening beggars? I thought they had powerful cameras trained on every inch of the streets. Perhaps like everyone else they just tape stuff and forget to watch it later.

Once the initial rush from the E has worn off I'm left with the lovely afterglow. But it's still not enough to shield me from the rigours of three and a half hours in the theatre. Perhaps the thrill will be surviving what Sasha thought would be a painful ordeal for me. She likes setting me challenges – custom certainly not staling *that* infinite variety of pleasure. And I have always liked Helen Mirren, who will be taking her clothes off. In the unlikely event of anyone asking her to play Mother Theresa of Calcutta or the Queen Mother, you would still put money on there being a nude scene. Not that she has to appear nude to get the work, as she is rightly adored by audiences and critics alike. But it does help to know there might be a reason to stay awake for the rest of the evening.

Milling about in the bar, I catch several besuited men attempting to have a good lech at Sasha without their wives noticing. She does indeed look radiant, wearing shiny new boots and a black rubber jacket well festooned with protruding rubber nipples and zippy bits. There was a time when she abandoned designer pervery, ever since civilians tried looking like sex outlaws, but tonight it's just right for distancing us from the theatre crowd. 'You look gorgeous,' I tell her.

Her eyes light up. I can still please her. Which is something. My pension plan might still be working.

'I bought some more shoes,' she says in a very quiet voice. She knows she's been naughty. We are not supposed to be mindless consumers these days. Sasha said so. 'But they're second-hand,' she pleads. 'Charity shop stuff.'

'Buy what you like. You look stunning.' She stands on tiptoes to push her face up to mine for a kiss – the way she did the very first time we met. I think there's a blue plaque now on Wimbledon High Street just by the tube to mark that kiss. That night I went home and did two hundred press-ups and still couldn't sleep at the prospect of what might be in store the next time we met. When we got drunk and fell asleep in each others' arms. Or did we? It's seven years and three murders ago now.

'I couldn't resist it,' she said of the new outfit. I start thinking about where she might have gone to buy it, if that could lead to word getting out that we are still alive and well. But then an electronic chime announces that it's time to be good little boys and girls and sit still for far too long.

It is probably superfluous to say that our seats are so far away from the stage there is little prospect of seeing anything. Added to which we are right in the middle of a posh school party. They just *love* Sasha's gleaming, glistening boots and shiny rubber jacket. They aren't as fond of the glowering bald man siring her, but I don't let that annoy me – or their inherited wealth. I am too busy coping with the fact that Prozac has turned my usually well-behaved digestive system into a furnace of churning gases. Like Cleo herself, I am all fire and air. While I am entirely successful in corking up my arse, the effort makes it even harder to tolerate the turgid goings-on down below on the stage when the play finally lumbers into motion.

It isn't working. Not happening at all. And for once I am not the only one who thought so. Helen Mirren is entrancing, as are her little group of minxes and handmaidens, but I'm pretty sure that when Antony finally falls on his sword it's not supposed to get a laugh. He really does stuff the sword in his armpit, trying to make it look like it was in his chest, exactly the way Morecambe and Wise used to do it in their admirably short little sketches. 'What? Not dead?' immediately after supposedly killing himself also teases out a few chuckles here and there. Even from the mile or so we are from the stage I still notice that he has time to carefully move a prop out of the way as he fell in apparent agony to the floor. There is also some general sniggering when epic battles are supposedly realised by three men staggering about holding non-existent wounds. Theatre actors still do drunkenness by falling about the stage while keeping their faces perfectly straight, which just looks phoney. Why don't I just say it looks *theatrical?* It looks fake, bogus, obviously not happening now or likely to happen, ever.

The staging is minimalist, making us do the work – thanks, mate. The music is horribly dated 1950s avant-garde percussion – random plinky-plonk xylophones and what sounded like a drunken rampage through a gong shop. It has precisely fuck all to do with the mystic East or sexual attraction or grand passion or the interminable boredom of Roman politics or indeed anything else, although it does prove that the composer must once have studied percussion and is at least fifty, probably older. Whenever the actors face the back of the stage I can't hear what they are on about and the English language seems to have evolved considerably since Shakespeare's day. Indeed, very little of it means what it used to, making it even harder to grasp what is going on. At least there is Sasha's perfume to be going on with, the proximity of her warm body, her sweet face and her wise eyes.

And when I get her back on E again, she will soon abandon

this mad scheme to annihilate the Dungeonmaster. I mean, in the general scheme of things what does a little vivisection matter? These days? Don't worry: I would never say that anywhere Sasha could hear. It would be more than my job's worth.

In the interval I see two women who look vaguely like Kate. But Sasha is still the ultimate. It's just a pity that reassuring her about our relationship means accompanying her on a journey to be killed somewhere cold and inhospitable. And all too soon we are back watching more shouting, arm-waving and running about. The plot could have been com-pressed into half an hour anyway. And why on earth a playwright with no funds for special effects or even scenery of any kind wanted to include a couple of sea battles is beyond me. People sometimes say films are slow if they take twenty minutes to get going. The first half of this play seems an awfully long way of saying that Antony fancied Cleopatra and some of his old chums didn't like it. Of course there are stunning passages on the page; that's why you buy your ticket in the first place. Then you find that, as you had always suspected, the worst film you have ever seen is better than anything in the theatre. And it's much cheaper. And you can see and hear everything. For most of the second half I am praying for the guy with the asp to show up and put her, and us, out of our misery. Most of the audience seem to agree. The concluding applause is less than ecstatic and is over in about twenty seconds.

'What did you think?' said Sasha, as we walk back alongside the river. The moon has never looked lovelier, Sasha never more radiant.

'Um, good,' I said cautiously. Sometimes people tell me I can be too negative. I didn't want to be accused of that again.

'Be honest,' she says.

'I don't think Antony looked very comfortable.'

'H'm. You don't like the theatre, do you? You were fidgeting a lot.'

'Well, I'm sorry I couldn't get better seats. We were a long way away.'

'I enjoyed it. Helen Mirren *rocks*.'

'Yes!' I say, glad to have the chance to say something positive for a change.

'At least you got to see her wrinkly old body,' she says.

'What?'

'You missed it? She changed into that shroud thing at the end.'

I remember closing my eyes to try to concentrate on the text. I had actually missed lovely, lovely Helen disrobing.

'I'd rather watch you any day,' I say, determined to salvage something from the evening. 'And I've been aching for you all day.'

'Those pills really work, don't they?'

'They work with people you're in love with.'

'Come on then, big boy. Let's hope Stefan's not in.'

And let's hope 'Stephanie' is.

But it turns out to be one of those evenings when Sasha wants to gang up on me with the nearest bystander. She doesn't want any E. She'd rather run me down in front of Stefan. As if this was some middle-class dinner party where women take turns to tell each other how crap their husbands are. While the men sit there and take it. Being a bit of a yob, I soon lose interest in that and storm out. I have my Ecstasy and the possibility that Kate might still be up. She might have gone out with some unspecified mates or she might be . . . I have no idea what she might do. Just that she isn't Sasha, which will do for the moment.

And I'm in luck. She's in, somewhere in Stockwell.

'Sorry it's late,' I say, on the second attempt. Perhaps this second E wasn't such a good idea. Although *I* can make sense of what I'm saying. 'What are you up to?'

'Work. But it's time I stopped. And opened a bottle of wine or two. How *are* you?'

Sometime later, after I thought I had summed things up rather nicely, she asks me if I'm all right.

'I've taken some drugs. I need to be with someone.'

'What's wrong with your wife?'

'Too much to tell you about right now. It's not going very well.'

'So come over.'

A licensed cab driven by a fat white clod stops for me. But then he changes his mind, seeing that I'm bald and pierced, obviously a poof. A pirate mini-cab then undertakes the journey for a fiver. Even better, the guy can't speak English so I can watch the bright lights flash past in peace. Kate has a first-floor flat in the badlands between Brixton and Stockwell, a decrepit building divided up into small people-hutches. The hall is dark and smells of cat wee and skunk but Kate looks ravishing – happy, healthy and unlikely to invade Bavaria in the near future.

Her rooms smell of herbs, garlic and plants. She has a wine rack and floor-to-ceiling bookshelves full of socialist books and magazines. Third World rugs and artefacts are littered about. She has a very expensive new computer and a tiny black and white television. And a brief root around the medicine cabinet finds a silver sachet of Prozac – one of the brands that Sasha and I briefly sampled before moving on to the next bogus panacea. She also has st john's wort and some little brown bottles of pills with long names with plenty of exes and zeds. Well, there had to be some explanation for why she was so attracted to me: she's mad.

'It's lively round here,' I tell her, when I'm seated with a camomile tea. For the third time in five minutes drum 'n' bass at club volume is booming out of a car at the traffic lights below. She rolls her eyes around her head.

'Lively! It's a field study in sexual harassment. The kids. Every time I go out I'm surrounded. If you don't say hello it's racist. They actually say that. If you do it's "Hello, baby! I'm the one for you". It almost makes you nostalgic for Bavaria. I might have to go back, actually. Munich, this time.'

'It's almost like you're following me,' I tell her.

Our eyes lock. I am soon aware that I had perhaps been assuming too much. She laughs at my disappointment.

'You're not *that* irresistible. I was there researching a programme about a mad scientist called Reinhard Adler,' she says.

Oh dear. Reinhard Adler, which may be the Dungeonmaster's real name – as far as anyone knows. She watches my face fall off with some amusement.

'He's some hideous Nazi who is trying to fuse the best parts of humans and animals to create, you guessed it, the new master race. I know all about Stefan's parents. Although I couldn't find anything on him.'

'He hates his parents. He might even be a liberal. He really isn't a Nazi.'

'And I looked you up too. Rob Powers' pianist. I know who you are. Your wife's a minor celebrity.'

All of a sudden I want to go home. How do I attract these people? Perhaps I should race model cars or go potholing.

Something domestic. Something more my level. 'You're a journalist?' I say.

She laughs, then covers her mouth. 'You should see your face. I'm an investigative journalist. Not that anyone gives a shit about that any more, but it's just something I have to do. Dad was a bit of a radical. Still is, really. I'd like to show him I can do it. And my smug bastard of a husband. I'd like to put *him* in his place.'

'What did he do?'

'We had a company. It was going to be an alternative news service. But he sold out. Fell for a rich bitch and her money. Now it's a fashion channel. Fashion!'

Now there's something we can agree on.

I should clam up now, but there's a chemical running around my brain telling me to do the exact opposite. And I'm aching for a hug. For some reassurance. For some sex, basically. But this is the wrong person. By any standards of anything. And to think she was prepared to use me just to help her career. Some people have no standards of morality. She offers me a coffee and I plead for decaff, as I'm probably already going to be up all night.

While she's gone fixing that I have a look at her bookshelves. It's hard to believe anyone can be bothered having this many books about politics. Although I understand completely why they are covered in dust. She has wedges of Noam Chomsky; maybe two hundred quid's worth of American feminism; a few books by their less-well-paid-and-not-too-happy-about-it English colleagues; and some titles by a socialist firebrand called Sam Lewis – who turns out to be her dad, according to the handwritten dedication inside. Then there's a lot of stuff about Israel, neo-Nazis and the Holocaust. Even *Time's Arrow*, Martin Amis's helpful attempt at making the Holocaust more interesting by running it backwards. Just in case it wasn't stylish enough the first time around. As her footsteps approach with a tray full of clinking cups it seems appropriate to try to say something about her impressive collection. Except that I'm the last man on earth to be able to offer an opinion.

'Antonio Gramsci, eh? Those were the days,' I start off, before realising that something a little weightier might be in order. But then my heart starts thumping. I need to get home and have a nice sit-down. For the next few years or so. She also has a copy of *Who Killed Rob Powers?* I pick it up and turn to confront her.

'I never got round to reading this. Is it any good?'

But I'm looking at an angry woman with a gun. She is standing in the approved stance of target-shooters and trained personnel the world over; weight distributed evenly and two hands to steady the weapon. Unfortunately I have to laugh. The rushes from the Ecstasy are starting, and the extra adrenalin kick is boosting the usually mild impact into something I can't cope with. Her face flushes red, as she thinks I'm laughing at her. Maybe I am, as even around here a gunshot would arouse some comment.

'Ever used one of those things before?' I ask.

'Yes,' she says. 'I'm a crack shot. I've won prizes. And you are a murderer and a Nazi and you climbed through my window to rape me. Shooting you will easily be worth the minor inconvenience of a trial. I'm bound to get off.'

'You're not going to shoot me. Even if that is a real gun.'

Her anger does look real though. Problem is, I don't care. Laughing out loud does nothing for her temper, but unless she's going to shoot me there's no point standing there with that gun. Now she thinks she's going to hit me with it, but it's easy to step aside the blow before it lands. You just wedge one hand in their armpit and disarm your assailant with the other. Sasha taught me one quiet evening in Bavaria . . .

When I wake up my head hurts. I have been expertly trussed up, face down on her dusty carpet. But this is not a games-playing scenario. Kate has metamorphosed into a hard-faced little tyke who has a snub-nosed automatic trained on me. It smells of oil, but not of cordite. She hasn't shot anyone recently. But that could change. Her eyes look flat and dead. And I have a mild Ecstasy comedown to cope with as well as the gradual realisation that Kate is not what she seemed.

'Water, I need water,' I tell her. No reaction. 'Please. I really need to drink something.'

'Tough.'

'Who *are* you?'

'It doesn't matter. But you're staying here for a while. Until a representative of the Rob Powers family gets here.'

Not him again. It's not fair. We didn't kill him anyway. It actually was suicide. Sort of. And we got away with it. It's history. As dead as her collection of musty old books about politics.

'You're in over your head,' I tell her, hoping that it's true.

'I chase Nazis. Then I kill them.'

'No, you don't.'

She shrugs. What does it matter what I say?

'You're just between jobs. And you've stopped taking your medication. Maybe that's why you're like this.'

'I really will shoot you if you say that. I'm selling you to the family of Rob Powers. There's a reward. Did you know? Does your wife know how easy it is to trace people on the

Internet? Or is she one of these hopeless cases who just wants to be famous? Even if it means getting caught?'

There's not much I can add to that.

'I have already e-mailed the Powers. They will arrange transportation to the airport.'

'This is bullshit. You can't fly unwilling passengers across the Atlantic.'

'You can if you have a private plane. And you will be unconscious.'

She's looking very pleased with herself.

'Once I found you were a pair of Nazis, that made it much easier,' she says. 'I get a million dollars and you two get what's coming to you.'

She looks a lot less cool now she is boasting. It's starting to look like one of Sasha's attention-seeking strategies. Look at me, Daddy. Love me. Or I'll kill you.

'We're not Nazis,' I tell her. 'Sasha wants to expose the Dungeonmaster too. She's as mad as you are. If you ask her nicely she'll tell you where his secret hideout is.' I'm croaking rather than talking by now. 'Look, I need water. I can't breathe.'

Kate doesn't care. She's been fooled before. Her heart's been broken. Her business has been ruined. She can cope with seeing me like this.

'Say you *can* deliver us to the Powers family,' I say. 'Are they really going to give you any money? Why should they? What are you going to do? Sue them? They have so much money they can't possibly lose. And it's all going to happen in America. By their rules.'

Her eyes don't flicker, her face stays the same but the ensuing silence must mean that she is chewing it over.

'Do you honestly think that Sasha would let you take us both back to America to face justice?' I ask after a while.

'How would she stop me?'

'She's a bit of a handful.'

'So am I.'

But not the sort of handful I was hoping for. The easy availability of Stefan must have made me careless. This is what happens when you abandon cynicism and start to embrace positive thinking. You get kicked in the teeth, every time.

'Don't go anywhere, will you?' she sneers, then pads off in her stockinged feet to the bathroom. Part of me wants to crawl along after her. But she has indeed tied me up very well. Not so well that I can't wriggle along the floor to where her phone is. Perhaps they didn't include that in her 'How to be a revolutionary socialist' night school course. But there's no time for the usual 'bitter reviling' that Sasha and Marcus Aurelius so rightly disapprove of. My life now depends on how long she will spend in the bathroom. And whether I can remember Sasha's new mobile number in this state. It started with two numbers in sequence. That bit's easy. Then 4646. 'For sex, for sex!' she said. 'It's a perfect working girl's number.' So it is. But the first digits are . . . something or other. I used an astrological mnemonic. Adds up to 22, which adds up to 4, which is the number of Cancer. 0976! Who said the occult was useless? Nudging her phone off the hook and tapping out the number with my nose comes right out of a worthless B-movie, finally justifying the thousands of hours I have spent slumped on the couch watching the box. I make a brief note never to stop watching television if I ever get out of here. The number is easy to tap out with my beaky nose, but I get the machine. Answer it! Pick it up! But there's no one there.

'Sasha. This isn't a joke. Kate's got me at 173b Stockwell Road. First floor. She wants the Rob Powers reward. You need to help. She's got a gun . . .'

Footsteps clatter back over bare floorboards.

'You fucking creep,' says Kate, running over to terminate the call.

'There's nothing you can do now,' I tell her.

Except hit me with the handle of her gun. Which hurts. For a while my shaved skull sings like a struck bell until the dust on her carpet triggers a thorough and comprehensive coughing fit. When this climaxes with retching and vomiting, Kate is finally moved to ask me if I'm all right. But I can't stop shaking, twitching from head to toe, while grunting incoherently. I appear to be dying, which is ironic really. Everyone will think this is some sex game that went wrong and I always hated being tied up. I can't breathe, excellent conditions for visionary trance work but also a fairly good indication of the approach of death. Tears stream down my face as I struggle for air, but there's nothing happening, nothing except slow suffocation.

If only my senses would allow me unconsciousness, but I have never felt more alive, more aware of the visions that start to shoot out from inside my eyes and bury themselves in Kate's swirling carpet. I can feel her boot in my side as she flips me over but watching her ceiling rotate seems just as final. I can't breathe. Even Kate is starting to look concerned. There is, after all, money at stake. Just as it starts to ease, some little sprite whispers in my ear that it might be worth continuing for a little while. And sure enough, Kate is moved to untie me. It's really not that hard to pick up her gun while that's happening. I can even flick the safety catch off.

'You bastard!' she says, not at all happy now. And then she

starts a fit of her own. Except this one's real. All of a sudden Kate is crying almost as much I used to when I was a drunk. Floods of tears, whining self-pity. It almost makes me ashamed to have tricked her.

But I didn't really want to go to America to be executed. Although there might be another fatality if she doesn't stop crying. It was harrowing at first; now it's annoying.

The first time I saw Sasha weep helplessly I wanted to rip my heart out and eat it, if it would make her feel better. Then I noticed that disputes tended to be settled in Sasha's favour whenever the tears flowed. It became her handy solution to everything. But at least with Sasha you were sure that it would be over pretty quickly. This looks permanent. Whatever will the neighbours think? If I wasn't such a gentleman I might feel like giving her a good shake to see if it would shut her up. She's rolled herself up into a ball now, rocking herself gently on her heels. There's never anything good to say at times like this. But I find the feeblest possible choice.

'What's the matter?' I ask. She howls on, turning up the volume a little, as some deep wellspring of grief is accessed. Or it could be that, like a lot of my playmates, she's just not very well. Well, I'm sorry but I don't feel like hugging her. She'll just have to pull herself together. Just as I'm tiptoeing towards the door she winds down with a cough and a splutter. A hard cruel face appears under the film of tears.

'I couldn't do it,' she says, bitter and self-hating. 'I had my big chance and I just couldn't do it.'

So it *is* self-pity. Something I can relate to.

'Isn't that something good? You're not bad enough to do this? Something to be proud of?'

'Oh, get out of here. Before I change my mind.'

Oh, yeah? But there's no time to taunt the tearful. It's time to go and do whatever Sasha says. For ever. 'You can still expose the Dungeonmaster,' I say. 'You could sell that idea to some network or other.'

She laughs out loud. 'Which commissioning editor is supposed to be interested in what some amateur scientist does somewhere in Bavaria? You can't even get anyone interested in *British* news. Never mind foreign stuff.'

'They love neo-Nazis. Scare stories about Germany.'

She walks up to me and cups her hand round my ear. 'Hello! Anyone in there? They can make a cheap programme about home improvements or a very expensive one about gene experiments somewhere abroad. They can make a docu-soap about some thick model. With guaranteed ratings. Or they can take on a rich man. And his private army. And an army of lawyers to go with it.' Her eyes are wild. Her hair is bedraggled.

'Whatever will they do?' she says, throwing her hands around until she finally finds a pose demented enough to express her anguish. 'I just can't imagine!'

'Where did you get the gun?' I ask her.

'Like I'm going to tell you! God, you're stupid!'

'There's not much point in having a gun if you can't even pull the trigger.'

'Yeah. I can't even kill Nazi scum like you!'

'I'm not . . . we are on the same side.' But she's not listening. She needs to change into a hairshirt and rub nettles all over herself.

'Look,' I say, 'Sasha wants to expose Reinhard Adler. He's supposedly sacrificing eight species of animal and a human being this Xmas. At some fortress in the Bavarian Alps. She's going to stop him. That's why we were staying at Stefan's.

She's an animal-rights fanatic. She'd do anything to stop this sacrifice.'

Her face has gone blank. Maybe, like me, she can't stand admitting she's wrong. But it doesn't look like I'm going to get another cup of camomile tea any time soon. It really is time to go.

Out in the street I say a little prayer to the moon, which is presently ripening up towards its big finish; the last of this year's thirteen full moons. Although I won't be really happy until I'm back at Stefan's. I want to see those moonbeams glinting on the dome of St Paul's. According to Sasha, Wren's masterpiece was built on the site of a perfectly good temple to the lunar goddess Diana. The Xians *would* rename a perfectly good feminine temple after a sex-hating misogynist. Westminister Abbey was the site of a solar temple, just in case you were wondering.

It seemed like a good idea to take the gun, until I spot a police car. It would be most unfortunate if I were to be one of the few white men ever to be stopped and searched in Brixton. Although I might well need a weapon if Sasha finds out what happened tonight. I ring her to cancel her arrival but she doesn't pick up. She's probably slept through the lot. And as soon as I have cabbed it to Stefan's I wipe my previous message off her phone as she lies twitching and stuttering. Our leader is much too busy to be bothered with inconsequential acts of treachery from the troops. Besides, I've seen enough frightening women for one day, what with that Cleopatra and now Kate. What Sasha doesn't know won't hurt her.

8

In 1875 the writer and occultist Guido von List climbed a hill overlooking Vienna to conduct a strange ritual. Von List was dedicated to returning greater Germany to an older, purer faith – the worship of Wotan and other pagan gods of the Teutonic race. Upon the hill he commemorated the summer solstice by burying a number of empty wine bottles, carefully arranged into a sacred symbol: the swastika.

Lucifer Rising by Gavin Baddely

SASHA HAS FOUND more information about the Dungeon-master on an anti-fascist website. My task today is to visit the magazine whose site it is and ask them everything else they know. While pretending to be a journalist.

It's easy. Sasha says so. 'You're spying on them!' she tells me. 'It'll be fun!'

'I remember the last time spying was fun. When I was in section two of *The Man from Uncle* fan club. I had a little card telling me what bit of the secret service I was in and a rifle with a shoulder stock in a black attaché case.'

'Cool!' says Sasha. 'I used to like Ilya Kuriakin.'

The blond one with the fringe. I used to look like that. When I was ten. When girls were divided into those who fancied Napoleon Solo, as played by the dark-haired Robert Vaughan, or the aforesaid Ilya Kurakin, as played by the blond David McCallum. As a child spy I wasn't sure that girls should be allowed on active service, but my pint-sized sister disagreed. I lost that battle, and I'm losing this one. The only difference now is that I have seen enough active service. I want to be invalided out. Retired hurt. Sat somewhere where you don't get shot at. With the other girls.

'What am I supposed to be finding out?' I ask her.

'Anything at all about the Dungeonmaster. Where these experiments take place. Where his secret hideaway is. But I'd prefer to see a picture of you as a happy little blond boy. What happened?'

'I really don't know. But I'm expecting to recover from my adolescence any minute now. Or at least before I die.'

'You'd better make a start then,' says Sasha. 'We haven't a chance against the Dungeonmaster. He's going to crush us like bugs.'

'Most amusing. Do I need a disguise for this mission?'

Her smile widens, as something particularly pertinent occurs to her. 'Buy the *Big Issue*. It might look like you care about anyone except yourself.'

'I care about you, my princess.' But she just sends me on my way with a kiss. And a gentle slap on the seat of my pants.

Looking in the mirror on the way out, I see an unshaven man whose face has been scraped off the street after a nasty road accident. Whoever stuck it back on again was probably drunk. Sasha finds the effect pleasing, but I have no idea why.

She is also under the impression that a drab like herself has been lucky to land a handsome blade like me. But she always gets logistical stuff right.

The *Beacon* magazine is exactly where she said it would be, in the bit of the East End yet to be developed. The crumbling office building also houses the remains of one of the Communist Party's splinter groups, now called something blatantly false and obviously misleading, like 'The Social Democratic Way' – just the sort of vaguely democratic title their Nazi opponents usually adopt.

John Booth is just as I had expected from his voice on the phone. He is hunched, dour and shabby, apart from his rusty-red, untrimmed beard. In my view bushy beards might be all right in Ireland or in the Old Testament, but they're not particularly helpful in the context of contemporary London. So I'm trivial. Sincerely held beliefs should matter more than surface sheen. Somewhere or other in the world there probably is someone who cares more about what a newsreader is saying than what he or she looks like. But not right now in London, and probably not in most other places either.

After one look at my kinky leather jacket and non-fashion combat pants, John Booth's welcoming smile becomes less than effusive. He does not spare me any of his Happy Shopper instant coffee. Nor do I get even a scrawny little roll-up from his well-worn tobacco pouch. He takes a Polaroid of me as I take a seat. Which leaves me with a bit of a dilemma. Tearing it out of his hands wouldn't look that good, and yet leaving it with him could lead to all sorts of complications. But the man is right to be suspicious. As far as he knows I am a journalist researching the Dungeonmaster. I have no proof of that. And my shaved head and leather jacket could of course blend in very nicely at any gathering of the Fourth Reich –

also at most gay clubs, both places where John's duff old leisurewear and beard would be rightly out of the question. I hand over the cash for all of his back issues. His face doesn't crack as he thanks me, his mumble barely fighting its way out of his beard.

'I'm writing an article on Reinhard Adler,' I tell him, or rather the side of his head.

He is staring out of the window, having already seen enough of me. He wants it to be known that he will be of as little assistance as possible and he is making a very good job of it.

'The Dungeonmaster,' says John. 'What do *you* know about him?'

'I know what he puts on the Net. The Aleister Crowley stuff. Trying to shock mummy and daddy while playing at being a Satanist. His occult dabblings.' I continue talking even though John is still staring out of his one grubby, smudged window. Heavy traffic rumbles past, shaking the building's foundations. 'He got deeper into the nationalist scene then came up with his grand synthesis of black magic and Nazi philosophy. Or reinvented the stuff which has been around since the early 1900s. Guido von List and all that. And business is booming.'

All John can see is stalled traffic and tower blocks underneath a slate-grey sky. He would still rather look at those than at me. I carry on talking anyway.

'Like Crowley, the Dungeonmaster has a massive ego and the wealth to gratify his every whim. He has climbed mountains in Tibet. He has published some poetry, not actually at his own expense. Unlike Crowley, the Dungeonmaster is an accredited chess grandmaster and a master of several martial arts.'

John turns to face me again. His face is slightly less hostile. 'Poetry? What's it like?'

He actually wants to know. Must be the beard, I suppose.

'The little I've seen is the usual fascist rubbish. Nature. Nietzsche. The cold bleak countryside, the strong warrior who follows his own path. Stuff about das Volk. The people,' I explain.

'I know,' he says, sounding about as weary as I feel. 'You seem to know a lot about it. How do I know you're not working for him?'

I shrug nonchalantly. I feel a persistent tremor in my cheek. Which can't look terribly impressive.

'If you're a journalist, where's your press card?' He says, leaning over the table. 'Who do you write for?'

'It's the alternative press. In Munich.' Where there is no alternative press. Everyone's too rich. Will he know that? He keeps on looking at me until I squirm, then relents.

'I'm going to give you the postbox address of a group of real socialists. The sort of people who know what to do with Nazis. They stopped the skins putting on a gig in Essex recently. Kicked the shit out of them. If you're a bullshitter, they will soon find out.' His tight little smile would seem to indicate that he would be delighted if I was to undergo a sound drubbing in the very near future. He has written the words Class Warriors on a scrap of paper with a familiar postbox address, the same one used by Odin's Knot. There is also a telephone number.

'Thank you,' I say. 'Hope you don't have to wait too long for the revolution.'

'Hope they don't kick your teeth out,' he says. But he doesn't sound all that convincing.

*

The Class Warriors are a small organisation. I would be surprised if they ever needed to put two tables together in the pubs where they plan their next punch-up. They have, however, sold large amounts of their incendiary rag, especially in book format, where their scurrilous parodies of the tabloid press make an amusing read. They get on the telly because of that medium's voracious appetite for any sort of extreme material, however fatuous. Even Jamie's been on the telly with his fetish morris dancing. But perhaps the Warriors are well known because of their networking skills and their ability as self-publicists. Jake Parker returns my phone call almost immediately.

'Do I know you, mate?' he says.

'I'm a journalist,' I say, perhaps unwisely. Soon there are justified waves of revulsion and hatred pulsing down the line. I let him tell me I am a cunt for a while before attempting to put the opposing view.

'Look, we are trying to expose the Odin's Knot mob.'

'I couldn't give a fuck, mate. For all I know you're just another middle-class parasite. All you lot ever do is try to make us look stupid.'

Which must be *so* hard. I mention that I will buy any number of drinks in exchange for information. Then he tells me to fuck off. Or perhaps not. He actually said 'Oh, fuck off!' but it soon becomes clear that this means 'Hang on a minute, mate. I must consider the immediate ramifications of this.' After a lot more swearing than you would think could ever fit into a simple exchange of information, he agrees to a meet in a pub. He somehow manages to make this sound like a brilliant inspiration, a spur-of-the-moment decision that might be a bit risky but will probably work.

'Where is it?' I ask, a note of genuine despair creeping into my voice. It's tough on the sober, watching what happens in pubs – the endless repetition, the pointless aggression, the darkness, the smell.

'Bethnal Green Road. The *real* East End. And you'd better be real, mate,' he says. 'We don't like people taking the piss.'

We fix the time and place and then it's time for me to scurry off to meet my boss. I want to be on time. It might just persuade her to show up less than an hour late occasionally.

'Do you want to meet some genuine white trash?' I ask Sasha.

'I'm white trash,' she says. 'Third generation. We just *have* to make a baby. I need your genes.'

'I am not of noble birth. I am the genteel poor. From the north. And then I got tattooed. So that's that. I can't even get a council flat. There's no one below me, babe. No one needs what I've got.'

'I do.'

'Well, good for you. Have you heard of the Class Warriors?'

'Are they communists?'

'No. Communists are always upper middle class for some reason. The one thing you can say about the Class Warriors is that they actually are working class. They just like street-fighting. And they hate the police.'

'So do I!' says Sasha seriously, and as she tries to look fierce I feel a great wave of affection sweep through me. 'Let's join up!' she insists, like a three-year-old who must immediately have whatever they have just seen on the telly. Or like me, come to think of it. There is definitely a problem with impulse control around here. Or should I say there is an issue that is proving pretty intractable. Sasha doesn't like me saying the word 'problem'. It's *so* negative. *So* British.

'Come on!' says Sasha. 'Let's *do* something for a change.'

'I don't think they have any women members, dear. They want bone-headed beer-drinking machines, always ready for a fight.'

'Just like you were when we met.'

'You always . . . ' I remember Sasha telling me that it is unhelpful to use these no-turning-back phrases like 'always'. And in the instant that this flashes up in front of me Sasha is back in.

'You killed a guy in a pub!' she says.

'Well . . . never mind about that. Anyone can make a mistake.' She shakes her head and returns to flicking through the TV channels. I don't know. Just because that guy's neck snapped easily, she seems to think I am some sort of a thug. And she started it anyway. Probably. I will never know, being blind drunk at the time. It's just a shame I can't tell the Class Warriors all about it. Given enough beer I'm as dumb and dangerous as they are.

'Do you reckon fifty quid might get us through an evening with some street-fighting men?' I am sorting through our stashes of currency.

'That's two rounds of beer, isn't it?' says Sasha.

'It might be quite reasonably priced in the pubs they drink in. As they're *working class*.'

'Why say it like that?'

'It should be obvious by now that no one class has any more value than any other. And what have they got to boast about anyway? The last time the working classes marched in support of anything in the East End it was Enoch Powell.'

Sasha looks puzzled.

'He was a blatant fascist who is still the hero of most of the British establishment. And all those lovable working-class East Enders, of course.' 'I love *EastEnders*!' says Sasha, meaning the soap.

I knew this already, but it's still as heartbreaking as finding a syringe hidden in your daughter's bedroom. 'And their looka-like bands and the Spice Girls and tabloid newspapers and voting three times for Margaret Thatcher,' I finish up. 'What have the working classes ever done for us?'

'You love working men's cafés.'

'Yes, but they would be even better if there weren't any builders in them. Then I could have my bacon sandwiches in peace.'

'Why not have your stewed tea and bad newspapers in your own home?' says Sasha.

'I couldn't. I just couldn't.'

She just shakes her head in despair. I can see her point. The English are beyond help. But at least we are going to leave more behind us than trillions of hamburger cartons and some Bruce Willis movies.

Sasha and I arrive at a pub tucked away into a piss-bedecked alley in Tower Hamlets. On one side is some derelict land bordered by corrugated iron and on the other a housing estate built in the 1950s. The pub is dark and smells slightly more of old smoke than fresh beer. There are posters advertising a music-hall night and a thirty-foot television screen showing football. My contact spots my shiny red boots and comes over. He is tall and thin, with white blotchy skin, brown hair that is long and lank and glasses with thick black frames. To add a touch of class he has gone for a stringy Zapata moustache that is very nearly brown. And not grey at all. Although it is grey enough to keep you looking back to check if he really thinks it's a good idea. His breath envelops us, confirming our suspicions that he might like a drink. And a fag to go with it.

'John Shaw?' he asks.

'Yeah. This is June Leah,' I tell him. This is one of Sasha's legal names, borrowed off a tombstone in Streatham. We once had to find new legal identities in a hurry, and the quickest way was to rob the dead. But it was quite a romantic evening actually, clambering over cracked tombstones and soaking up the rays from a full moon. Cheaper than dinner and a movie anyway.

'You didn't say you was bringing anyone,' says Jake. As if I have committed a breach of security.

'I'm his wife,' says Sasha, something she occasionally takes a perverse delight in saying. 'He tells me *everything*.' She watches me trying to look as if this is true and then smiles, winking at me to let me know she can see right through me.

The old man having been dispatched, she smiles brightly at our host. He can't cope, and I'm not surprised. She has such a warm smile. But why is it being used on such an unworthy recipient?

In the corner are the rest of the Class Warriors, already shouting at each other although it is eight-thirty, still another two and a half hours of pub time to go. And then the lock-in. You might see these men propping up any bar where the sub-human go to watch football before a kebab on the way home. Horrible anoraks, cheap trainers, risible hair and the sort of faces that weren't pretty even before they were battered flat. Amazingly enough, no women have showed up tonight, so Sasha is the only civilising influence on the premises. We can't count the barmaid because she is ladling out the beer. And she should be up on a charge of incitement to riot, the way this lot drink. Her face and upper body glow with fresh perspiration as she struggles to keep up with the orders. She still has time to scrutinise our faces as Sasha and I both order tomato juice. Are we ill? Or on something else?

'So what do you want?' asks Jake, once we have joined their table.

'We're after a guy called the Dungeonmaster,' says Sasha, 'a powerful European Nazi who funds the skinhead music scene. And the Black Metal bands. We're looking for people to help us stop him.'

Jake turns bright red and starts spitting at us. This is not pointless exaggeration for supposedly humorous effect. His face actually is bright red, and there is genuine working-class spittle spraying on Sasha and me as he talks – at considerable length, jabbing at us with a nicotine-stained finger every now and again.

' . . . you think you can just come down to the East End and buy us off? You yanks are all the same. You come over here—'

'—and take our jobs,' I say, because it's what bigots used to say about immigrant workers. Jake's dad may have said it. What is immediately certain is that *I* shouldn't have just said it. His face freezes, and some of the nearby banter quietens down as people realise we could at last be getting down to it: a fight, the reason for living. Jake slams his pint down and points a finger at me.

'Listen, cunt,' he says, but Sasha is in before he can get any further.

'We are on the same side,' she says, holding up both hands, palms outwards.

'We both want to get the Dungeonmaster. I mean, from an animal rights point of view what he is presently planning . . . It's so disgusting and barbaric. He must be stopped.'

Sasha, Sasha, Sasha. These people eat fried animals three times a day. Like I do, whenever I get the chance. But as it turns out, I'm completely wrong.

'What do you mean?' says Jake, forgetting to drink in the heat of the moment.

'There is an ancient Norse tradition of sacrificing nine species of animals, including a human being, to mark midwinter. It's meant to fire the sun up again. The cover for this event is a battle re-enactment. A winter tournament for his brave Vikings.'

'We could go over there and 'ave them,' says a young man with a glass scar around his eye. There is some tutting and headshaking from the older, wiser men.

'They are armed neo-Nazis who train together under cover of battle re-enactment,' says Sasha. 'The only safe thing would be to get in undercover.'

'What?' I shouldn't have said that probably, but the full horror of this plan is only just starting to be revealed.

Sasha winks at me before continuing: 'This year's special because the Nazis are doing well all over Europe. But he doesn't care about democratic politics because he is financing experiments on animals and maybe even humans. Gene manipulation. It's the same old shit. Creating the next master race.'

'Right,' says Jake, glugging a heroic three inches of lager. 'And you're going to do something about it?'

'I'm putting together a small group of committed animal-rights people and anti-fascist—'

'—I got into the Warriors from hunt-sabbing,' Jake says.

'The people I really admire are the Animal Liberation Front. They're *radical*.'

His mates are less than impressed.

'You just fancy her,' says one of the beer-disposal machines before dipping his face to Sasha. 'Sorry, love.'

Sasha doesn't take offence, even though it is an unsolicited endearment. She can tell that this noble knight fancies her too. Most of the Warriors appear to have come to a decision about Sasha by now. They think she's cracked. But lovely. And they might be right. Meanwhile, Jake is hanging on her every word.

'Well, I'm looking for people to help me destroy this guy,' says Sasha. 'Let's recap. He's a rich Nazi. And a factory farmer. And a vivisectionist. And because he's into black magic he tortures farm animals and drinks their blood.'

Like you used to, dear. When you were a teenager. It was only once, but you killed an animal and drank its blood. You did. Nothing you do now will ever change that. It's not the right moment to share that with the group, so I lumber off to get more beer and two tomato juices, colliding with a very badly placed table as I do so.

When I get back Sasha is still motivating her troops. 'I need street-fighting men. People experienced with weapons. You need to be prepared to kill, if necessary.'

There is something like a hushed silence after she has said this. They can see she means it. They can tell she isn't just a rich thrill-seeker. She is obviously as mad as they are. But then something happens on the big telly screen and it's footie time once more. When they've stopped swapping football-based banter we return to the matter in hand: the quenching of several ferocious thirsts. I was bored when we arrived. One more hour of this and I'm ready to hitch back to Bavaria to check out the church bells. But there's no doubt Sasha has a live one here.

'There's only one thing to do with fascist scum like him,' Jake is saying. 'Give 'em a taste of their own medicine.'

There is much rattling of pint glasses, and horrible bloodthirsty oaths are exchanged. The lads are ready for battle. And most of them don't even know who they will be fighting. It's almost enough to arouse the suspicion that they might just like fighting for its own sake. But that can't be true. They are obviously motivated by the unequal distribution of wealth and the exploitation of the poor. There is, however, only one man Sasha gives her mobile number to.

And Jake folds the number carefully before putting it in a battered leather wallet next to his travelcard and his Arsenal season ticket.

'We're having a strategy meeting tomorrow,' she whispers. 'In Crystal Palace. Why don't you come? There are three of us already. But we need *you*.'

Her eyelashes flutter. Jake loses it immediately, as well he might, while I blunder off towards the door. I'm not even sure if she will follow, but a patter of high heels eventually joins me in the alley and we can get back to Stefan's.

'Did you have to seduce him?' I ask next morning. 'He would have done it for the money.'

'I don't want mercenaries. I want people who believe in the cause.'

'So what's Stefan doing?'

'Leading us to the Dungeonmaster.'

'He doesn't know where he is.'

'I think he's lying. And once we get him on his own we will get the truth out of him.'

Our eyes lock. Time stands still as we come to an unspoken agreement about a spot of non-consensual torture. Nothing gruesome, you understand. Just the pushing of boundaries. Perhaps the gentle easing into a tight musky orifice of insistent springy bits of black bulbous silicone. The utilisation of a certain strap-on for the purposes of interrogation. Once we have taken him into a light trance by a preliminary scourging. Sorry, mustn't get carried away. But for the first time there is something to look forward to on this mission.

Crystal Palace was recently the site of a long battle between developers and a surprising coalition of eco-warriors and sub-urban residents. The locals weren't that keen on an enormous cinema and fast-food complex, and the council were insistent that they should have a choice of twenty screens all showing Americans blowing each other up. To accompany this vital new arts venue, there will be all the popcorn and hamburgers you could possibly eat. All set in a lovely new shopping mall and parking space for a thousand vehicles. Well worth the destruction of a park and a few kids getting run over.

This long, bitter battle may be why the old bag behind the café counter stares at us with such venom. We have facial piercings. We must be eco-warriors. But it may be because we are customers. Service-users do tend to get in the way of the smooth running of a retail outlet, and we are no exception. It's lucky Stefan's busy today because then we would be Nazis too. Although for once the kneejerk reaction of the English to anyone German would be appropriate.

'Do you have vegetarian breakfasts?' asks Sasha.

'Vegetarian breakfasts?' The woman behind the counter is overworked and underpaid. But the real issue is jealousy of beautiful young Americans.

'Mushrooms, scrambled eggs, tomatoes, toast, no butter, and two black coffees,' says Sasha. I'd love a full English heart attack myself, but I'm going to order in solidarity with the wife.

'It's tinned tomatoes!' says the woman triumphantly.

But that won't stop Sasha. The tussle continues until Sasha gets her order written down on a pad and eventually two bitter cups of stale filter coffee arrive. But this black, bitter brew has nothing on Jake when he arrives.

'Hangover?' I ask, after he has wound up our hostess with an order for really strong tea.

He spends some time trying to make us feel as grumpy and hungover as he is but nobody wants to play. Then Jamie bustles through the door in a green tartan kilt, a studded leather jacket and a T-shirt announcing to anyone who can still read that he is a pervert. There is a stitched leather cylindrical backpack slung over his shoulders. It's a dramatic entrance, one more befitting Errol Flynn playing Robin Hood than a man entering a café in Crystal Palace. Sasha and I like it, but you can tell Jake isn't particularly impressed.

'Pleased to meet you,' says Jamie, holding out his hand and insisting on a shake even though Jake doesn't want to. Jake keeps his sulk going despite Jamie's painfully infectious bonhomie.

'Spent last night thrashing a maiden with a sjambok . . .' he starts, to Sasha's evident approval and to a slightly bewildered look from Jake.

'The South African riot police use them. Right?' asks Sasha.

'Indeed so. It's a versatile instrument. A flexible sabre really. Does everything from a kiss to decapitation . . .'

Sasha's giggling again. I'm smiling. For once. But whether

there should be so much hilarity engendered by the admittedly entertaining Jamie is debatable. *I'm* certainly going to carry on debating it anyway. Even if I have to do it all by myself. This is one of the few things I'm really good at – stomping around muttering and swearing. Visualising the painful deaths of my enemies. Moaning and groaning in public. And to think some people call this madness. Jake is having the same problem with the infinitely self-assured Jamie. He tries to head us off into Class Warrior territory. Which is only fair, as he has listened to our stuff. But it's not playing well. None of us wants to know. And Jamie says just the wrong thing when he brings back another round of teas.

'Here,' says Jamie, 'you have the chipped mug. It suits you.'

Jake doesn't like that. But there's nothing he can do about it. Jamie is tougher and cleverer. But there's always me.

'What's lover boy doing here?' he asks Sasha. 'Is he training?'

'I might watch,' I tell him. 'I could do with a laugh.'

'Oh, come on,' says Jamie. 'It'll do you the world of good.'

Fortunately Sasha chooses this moment to flourish a bag of goodies bought from the second-hand leather shop a few doors down from the café.

'Look what I got!' she says, smiling broadly while the men start to shift in their seats, dreading the deadly tedium of what's coming next. Shopping – so much more creative than actually making anything up. Sasha knows we couldn't care less but still insists on showing us a small purple leather handbag. She even models it, smiling winsomely while displaying it over one hip then the other. The interest is not the design, its purpleness or its lustrous gleam. It is interesting because Sasha has just bought it. Unfortunately this is not a theory that stands up to logical analysis, although Jamie and

Jake can still manage to admire it – both probably wishing to delve into various of Sasha's dark secret places one of these days. She has also bought a swagger stick. And a jumble of loose-fitting combat gear which will go well with her knee-length boots.

'The chief,' I say, trying to find her a new name. One befitting this new military persona. 'The boss. The general.'

'Chief of staff,' she says, using her fingertips to stroke the length of her swagger stick. Then she slowly wraps her lovely lips around the bulbous gold tip of her 'staff'.

'It's a pun,' she tells me, pointing at her 'staff' frantically, believing my stone face to indicate that I have missed the cream of the jest.

'I know,' I say wearily. She makes her eyes cross into each other and then increases the pace and force of her phallic thrusting until we have full-on simulated fellatio. Her silly cross-eyed face makes me laugh, mostly because it's evidence that she might not be completely mad at the moment. There is still hope. But the woman behind the counter is not amused.

'Right, you lot. Out!' She rumbles over, brawny forearms bared, her face as purple as a baboon's bum. 'Get out! Get out now!'

'Great Scott, woman. I haven't had my breakfast,' says Jamie.

She storms back to the counter, leans her considerable bulk on the till and then scrabbles around in it until she has found the price of Jamie's fried egg and mushrooms. She lumbers back over then slams it on the table. 'Come on! Out! Or I'm calling the police!'

Very soon we are on our feet and on our way. Taking on the Dungeonmaster is one thing. But there's no point starting a fight with a woman like this.

'I bet you're squatters, aren't you?' says our hostess. 'Never done a day's work in your life.'

'I served in the Falklands, madam,' says Jamie. He rolls up his shirt and shows her what may be a regimental tattoo for all I know. It's an official-looking crest anyway.

'Well, what are you doing hanging about with this lot then?' She waves a big red arm at 'us lot'.

'Shut up, you old bag,' says Jake.

She clips his ear. There is a lot of weight behind that arm and all of it landed on the side of Jake's head. He freezes, then pulls his arm back in readiness for a knockout punch. Jamie is so quick I can't quite understand what he has done, but all of a sudden Jake is accompanying Jamie out of the door in an armlock.

'And a good day to you, madam,' says Jamie.

Sasha and I follow, eager to find out why Jake has become so docile all of a sudden. Once we are on the street we can see that Jamie also has Jake twisted around by his little finger.

'I'm going to let go now,' says Jamie, 'if you promise not to get us arrested. Some of us have Dungeonmasters to kill. Dragons to slay, that sort of thing.'

He releases Jake, whose customary veggie pallor has turned crimson.

'I'm sorry, mate, but we had to get you out of there,' says Jamie.

Jake can only bluster as we walk through the traffic-choked streets to the park.

'What's in there?' I ask Jamie, nodding at his backpack.

'This? Sometimes it's a quiver full of arrows. Sometimes it's full of whips and canes. And today it's full of swords.'

'Stuff you made?' asks the shining-eyed Sasha.

We enter the park from the northern gate, passing through

a prissy little garden before walking down a bare hillside until we find a place where we might be able to play undisturbed. Unfortunately it's also a place from where we can see cowed husbands and proud single dweebs racing foot-long formula-one replica cars. There is a figure-of-eight track built especially for this purpose. It's not a particularly proud moment to be a man. Sasha looks as if she is going to say something about men's hobbies then swallows it. Before deciding to say it anyway.

'It's typical . . .'

'Go on,' I say. 'Men are all idiots because some of them have stupid hobbies.'

'I was going to say that it's typical you can't get a decent coffee in a park this size. I was going to ask if we should get some coffee.'

Her smile is tight-lipped but not necessarily the start of a long bitter feud. If I do something about it right now. So I stumble off in search of some coffee. And perhaps carrot cake for the little lady. Which will just have to do. I'm certainly not saying 'sorry' out loud. The search takes me past some life-size dinosaurs and a lot of grizzling children and tired parents. All things considered, it could be worse. At least Sasha's given up trying to reproduce. When I eventually return with the drinks Jamie is unscrewing a small hip flask.

'Come on, laddie. Have a wee dram.'

I look at Jamie, but it's clear that he has forgotten the ten previous times I told him we can't drink. I just shake my head and watch as he takes a slug from his silver flask.

'Pipe?' He is tapping skunk into a credit card-shaped smoking implement. Its internal labyrinth keeps the smoke cool so you can melt more of your brain before your lungs give out.

'Can we train after that?' I say, watching him suck the smoke in.

He holds up one finger to signify there will be a short pause. When he has finally expelled the smoke he can talk once more.

'It sharpens you up,' he tells me. 'If you're fit in the first place, of course.'

'I'd better not then,' I tell him.

'Two weeks of basic training will sort you out, laddie. It's a shame we're off before the weekend. The Hounds of the Morrigan are taking on the Viking Hordes.'

'What's that about?' says Jake, his ears pricking up at the news of a pointless drunken brawl.

'Mostly the consumption of copious amounts of strong drink,' says Jamie. 'And scourging maidens by the light of the full moon. If you're lucky.'

I wish Sasha wasn't smiling. No danger of Jake's scowl disappearing though.

'Not that re-enactment bollocks,' he says.

'You'd love it,' says Jamie. 'I'll take you along. I'm a member of the Dark Ages Society, the Hounds of the Morrigan, the Viking Hordes and the Men of Essex. The Dark Ages Society is great fun. Putting the sword to the Saxons. Who are all poofs, of course.'

'You're wearing the kilt, mate,' says Jake. 'Only poofs wear kilts.'

'Methinks you protest too much,' says Jamie. 'Have a blunt sword.'

'Uh?' says Jake, and I'm with him on this one.

Jamie reaches into his pack and hands him a sword with a blunt point. 'Now we can train without killing each other,' says Jamie, leaping up on to a nearby rock. 'Have at you!'

Jake hefts his sword and they are soon happily engaged in a pitched battle. Up hill and down dale. There is much banter and badinage centred around the other's predilection for taking it 'right up the arse'. Jake says this so often, and with such relish, that you would almost think he fancied it himself. But that can't be right. He's a fighting man.

'You come here with your bloody skirt on,' he's telling Jamie, as their swords clank together. 'And your hairy legs.' Jamie jumps back to dodge a clumsy thrust. 'And your porridge,' continues Jake, out of breath now. 'Which you can shove *right up your arse*! Along with the rest of Scotland. You're just a girl. A fucking woman.'

I look to see how our queen is taking this monstrously unacceptable statement. But she is smiling back happily at me. Perhaps realising that tough guys have to be like that. After all, if soldiers, football fans and gangsters could cuddle up with each other they wouldn't want to scrap. And then where would we be? The whole economy might grind to a halt.

'Happy, babe?' I ask. 'You're pulling the strings again. The puppets are dancing. To your tune.'

'Yeah! We have a posse,' says Sasha.

'Yes. We have our "homies",' I say. She knows what's coming but she's too happy to stop me. 'Look, it's embarrassing when dumb teenagers pretend to be LA gangbangers. Why would *you* want to do it?'

'Posse is a perfectly good word,' she says, in the voice she uses to tell me to eat my tofu. 'You know what you're doing? You're just like the Dungeonmaster. You're trying to control the language. You want every single word to be Germanic. No slang, no degenerate French or Latin.'

'What?'

'Real Nazis try never to say any word which isn't of Germanic origin. Nothing French. Nothing Latin. *You* sound just like them. If I want to use black street slang I'll use it. You're just another Nazi. About being English.'

I can't think of why she's wrong just this minute but she is. Meanwhile the boys are still skirmishing. Jamie is very nimble. As for Jake, we might as well ring the ambulance now. But he's game, I'll give him that.

'So Queen Sasha found her knights. Brave warriors who would sacrifice their lives for her.'

'Would they?' she says, wide-eyed and gooey.

I nod over towards the swordsmen. Jamie is now thrusting and parrying with an imaginary opponent as Jake pukes his breakfast up.

'Nice,' I say, as I tend to do whenever my sensibilities are offended. Sasha chuckles earthily. Maybe I'm a girl and she's a bloke. And her sly expression would seem to indicate that she has a few thrusts and parries ready for me.

'What's the difference between the legend of King Arthur and some rapper pretending to be brave and heroic?' she asks. 'They're both fictions.'

I open my mouth and find I have nothing to say. So I busy myself collecting the empty cups.

'I haven't finished that,' says Sasha, rather too frantically. 'Don't mess everything up! You always do that . . .'

'Aha! We're not supposed to say "always".'

'No. It's just you who can't say it.'

Jake has now progressed to retching up thick yellow bile while Jamie is giving his ghostly adversary a really hard workout.

'It's nice to see the kids playing,' says Sasha.

There are dangerous undercurrents in that deceptively

simple remark. She will have to be steered away from the subject of procreation.

'And that's going to defeat the Dungeonmaster?' I ask.

'And Stefan,' she reminds me. 'Our Trojan horse. He will take us to the Dungeonmaster. It's perfect. I am a natural-born leader.'

'Der Führer,' I say, but this inappropriate comparison just triggers a grin. 'Wouldn't it be "die Füehrerin"?' she asks.

'Doesn't sound right. What about "Supreme Ogress Sasha"?' I ask. 'That certainly used to work.'

'Not very military, is it?' she says. And she's serious.

'It's your father, isn't it? Just because he was a soldier.'

I stand back and wait for the tears. I had honestly thought that was a knockout blow. She would weep, I would kiss her better, then we would call the whole thing off. She's supposed to hate her father, you see. At least that's what she's been telling me all these years.

'My dad wasn't all bad,' she says. 'I just wish I could see my mom. You know. One last time.'

There is a pause I'm supposed to fill with sympathy or useful advice, but I don't know anything that would help, about that or anything else. Luckily Jamie is off on another swashbuckling performance – leaping from one rock to another while bellowing nonsense at all that empty green space. It will be such a relief when the Tory scum cover it in concrete. I'm not entirely sure why he needs to be cracking a fifteen-foot bullwhip, but luckily Jake has taken on the role of straight man.

'What's that?' he says, scowling less now as Jamie's charm is starting to take effect.

'Kangaroo hide,' says Jamie, stroking the coiled, light brown leather. He caresses the gleaming length of premium-quality hide lovingly – partly because he made it himself and partly because it conjures up pleasant memories.

'Can I have a look?' says Jake, the first time I've seen him say anything remotely deferential to Jamie. I suppose he might respect anyone who can make something that actually works. Rather than those who are content to rest on past glories. Like myself.

'Why isn't it black?' says Jake.

'It's kangaroo hide. This is a stockman's whip. Australians use it to drive recalcitrant cattle around the vast space of the Antipodes. It's a useful way of clearing a space for yourself.'

Soon he is cracking the long whip over one shoulder then the other. He throws the whip to his right, then his left. It cracks mightily, both times. The crack resounds over the slope all the way down to somewhere frightfully nice in Surrey and back again. Once Jamie's shirt is off we can see his whipcord muscles twist and knot as the bullwhip cracks.

'I may be the most adept whip-handler in the northern hemisphere,' he says, self-mocking, but even so . . . it's not *really* a joke.

I watch Sasha watching Jamie. She is in awe of the whip cracks. And the wisecracks. And I can see why. Jamie stops cracking his whip long enough to notice that I am slumped against a rock. And not running around honing my primordial killing instinct.

'Come, come,' he says. 'We need brave warriors. Fighting men who will stop at nothing until we find our grail.' He throws an arm out to emphasise that what we need now is derring-do. And not derring-don't, which is what I am supplying.

'Can't I be the mascot?' I ask. 'The regimental goat or something?'

He hauls me to my feet. And soon we are running around in circles again. Don't tell anyone, but it's quite enjoyable once you start. Then it becomes uplifting. A voice inside me whispers that I could have been happy all these years if I had heeded my father's advice. Less gloom and doom and more exercise. Perhaps Sasha's investiture will inaugurate a new era in which I become a man, instead of a frightened little boy. But I doubt it somehow.

'Same thing tomorrow,' says Sasha, once we are all flat on our backs watching the sky rotate. 'And this time we'll make Stefan do it too.'

'Will he be sitting on his arse as usual?' asks Jake, sneering at me.

It's true I had to be excused after a little while, but you have to build up slowly in basic training. Sasha turns an inquisitive eyebrow on him. Very soon he is looking at the floor.

'Matt collected all the information on the Dungeonmaster,' she says. 'He found out how to nick his mail. And that's why we know the location of the winter tournament.'

Which was news to me. But my heart swells anyway. I never knew she could be so loyal.

'He should be able to use a sword though,' says Jamie.

'So show me,' I say, dragging myself to my feet. I was dreading this, but swordplay turns out to be quite good fun. Until the arrival of the police. We have about ten seconds to think up a good story as a young copper approaches. Why are we engaged in paramilitary manoevres? Can I even remember which identity we are using presently? There is just time to shoot Jamie an astral deathbolt before he is upon us.

'Do you know it is an offence to carry dangerous weapons?' says the stripling who appears torn between duffing up Jake and nodding respectfully at Jamie. Then he spots Sasha for the first time and his vision momentarily blurs. The ghost of a slinky 1950s alto saxophone motif sounds in his head. His vision has misted up, and it appears likely that his testicles have just switched to flat out sperm production.

'Sorry, officer,' says Jamie. 'They're just play-swords. No points. We have a charity event coming up, you see. The Dark Ages Society are having a sponsored medieval weekend. It's for an educational trust. We have to survive in the wilds of Essex for forty-eight hours with only dried meat and strong ale.'

'These are dangerous weapons,' says the boy. But they are also toys he wants to own.

'Sorry, officer. I don't wave this thing around when civilians are present. I forged it myself. It's a simple process of . . .'

Five minutes of earth time pass as those of us without an interest in sword-forging experience something like the dawn and passing of the said Dark Ages. It soon becomes clear that Jamie has probably gained another recruit for his running-around-dressed-like-prats society. Every now and again the policeman steals another look at Sasha, even though he doesn't want to miss a word of the sword-forging workshop. Yes, she's still that beautiful. No, you can't show her your truncheon. But I need not hurl an astral deathbolt at him because this perfectly decent young man has been charmed by Jamie. He wishes us good evening as he strolls off.

'There you are,' says Jamie. 'Even the police like us. It's a good omen.'

'I really need that drink now,' says Jake.

Sasha gives him such a look that he is very soon staring at the ground between his feet like a well-chastised slave. She quickly glances over at me to see if I have noticed this new manifestation of her awesome power. I incline my head as if to say 'Well done, dear' and then she returns to drilling her troops.

As the stern talking-to continues it becomes increasingly clear that there may be some dispute about my status as official observer. I am going to have to fight. There may not be a vacancy for a regimental mascot. We don't need a war artist or a company bugler. We are all knights, ready to serve Queen Sasha. That's what she says anyway, and I'm not going to disagree.

'It is time for you all to kneel,' says Sasha. Although she is holding Jamie's sword it is the look on her face and the sound of her voice that make the three of us kneel in a circle around our queen bee.

'This is a symbolic beheading,' says Sasha. Which makes me breathe a little easier. You just never know with my little Sasha. 'Once you have agreed to serve me you have truly "lost your heads".' It's a relief to hear her finally come out into the open with it. We wait in reverent silence. Oblivious of the traffic, the distant car alarms, the thick teenagers and their mobile phones and a mad old woman with five yappy dogs. Any competent sorcerer could tune that lot out. But I'm out of practice. Until Sasha starts the sort of banishing ceremony that goody-goody witches use — except she has chosen the colder Nordic liturgy.

'Hammer in the north, hammer in the east, hammer in the south, hammer in the west.' We intone the words, visualising the symbol as we do so.

'Repeat after me: "We each undertake to defeat the Dungeonmaster or die in the attempt".' I repeat it along with the troops. But I'm thinking of my contingency plan. Which involves giving our leader a massive dose of E. Once she's felt the love-wave wash over her she won't want to go anywhere near the Dungeonmaster's winter sacrifice.

9

'WE'VE GOT TO do something about those bells,' I tell her.

'Stop whining!'

We're back in Bavaria. Preparing for the assault on the Dungeonmaster. It's Xmas fever in the village, ten masses a day rather than three and the bells they are a-ringing.

'Try and calm down,' she says. 'You're making yourself ill.'

I have indeed lost my mind. London taxis are not really designed for thousand-mile journeys. But it did get our gun and our drugs through the non-existent security at Calais. Unfortunately there is no peace and quiet in which to recover from the rigours of the journey – just the endless clanking and tolling of the bells.

Sasha is back in her combat gear, as we prepare for the final assault: leather jacket, khaki trousers and a quick-release holster for Kate's automatic. I know we argue a lot, but this is ridiculous. She doesn't really need to be armed for domestic disputes.

'I'm going to do something about those bells,' I tell Sasha as they toll relentlessly on. 'I can almost feel my bones ringing,'

I tell her, although she appears distracted by something rather more pressing.

'Have you done your hundred press-ups and sit-ups?' she asks.

'Yes, ma'am.'

'Well, cheer up then. And no church-burning before the winter tournament.'

'It's easier for them. Norwegian churches were wooden rather than stone . . . '

'I don't care! What do you think we should be? I don't know whether to be Nordic or Germanic.'

'With a name like Kristinson shouldn't you be a Viking?'

'And you should be a surly native. Gone soft. Ripe for a spot of rape and pillage. Just as you were when I found you.'

'Did Stefan get us those passes to the winter tournament?'

'So he says. And he arranged the Brotherhood of Saturn forgeries. I wrote the text and Stefan had it done for me.'

I can't share her euphoria here. Surely forgery is harder than that? Change the subject.

'Why is it called a winter tournament? I thought it was a sacrifice.'

'Hello! They don't tell people they're about to kill someone. The cover story is a real tournament. A little bit like re-enactment but without the battle. Jousting. Wrestling. Archery. The martial arts.'

Sasha's eyes are sparkling. Mine are probably doing their usual imitation of the cold blue lakes in which Odin's sacrificial victims were once bound and strangled.

'You're not entering?' I ask.

'No way. I'm a lady. It's the knights who get killed. And hurry up!'

'What?'

'Stefan fixed a meeting with Werner Stettner. He checks people out before they get to meet the Dungeonmaster. Nazis are usually uptight about arriving on time.'

Just an hour later my little ice-maiden is ready. Sasha's hair is twined around her ears in tight concentric circles, a German fashion that has so far failed to travel anywhere else. She is wearing brown and green linen – good rustic Nazi colours – set off by a National Partei Deutschland lapel badge and runic earrings. The meeting is in a dark underground bar decked out with swords, stone arches and heraldic motifs. The waitresses are sturdy. Meat and bones feature heavily on the menu. Its biker clientele wears skull-and-crossbones badges and tattoos. These men are anything but skeletal. Well fleshed and well refreshed, they drink standing up, clustered round huge barrels on which they rest their ample girths. Heavy Metal plays on a jukebox, which features the American Confederate flag. It's smoky and noisy, but Jake and Jamie seem perfectly happy at the prospect of an afternoon drink with the boys. They are less happy once they have seen legs of pork and ribs of this and that, but we are supposed to be undercover. With some reluctance they leave out the veggie rant and we survive the first ten minutes of our mission – considerably longer than I expected.

But we still have to impress Werner Stettner – the real Dungeonmaster's Apprentice, as some bloke on the Internet said, according to Sasha. Can this untidy-looking blond giant really be him? He is presently bellowing into his 'handy' – a German term for a mobile phone, derived from English as many of their new words are. His huge pale face is scarred and pitted. His long blond hair is all over the place, in 'Zigeuner Ordnung', as the locals sometimes say (messy like

Gypsies). His nose has been repeatedly flattened. He is somewhere in excess of six and a half feet tall. And I have forgotten
to use metres again, which is apparently less ageing.

Just in case his slabs of muscle and fat aren't intimidating
enough, he has bulked himself out with a leather waistcoat
and a baggy combat jacket. There is no fashion for combat
gear in Germany, the locals being a bit sheepish about their
recent heritage. But Werner isn't concerned about looking like
a liberal. The patches on his jacket refer to the SS, the KKK
and the English Oi! movement, whose skinhead rock predated
the fashion for Nazi noise by a good few decades. He is
smoking Marlboro from a soft red pack. Each man has an
open pack of cigarettes either in front of him or in the top
pocket of his work shirts. Should anyone ever run out of
cigarettes they dive into their comrade's pocket, which pro-
vides another welcome opportunity for a mock fist-fight.
Werner's wheat beer has been served in an imitation glass
boot that holds two litres of beer. And yet it fits snugly into
his huge fist. Werner's call finishes with many an affectionate
'Leck mich Am' – Kiss my (. . . arse). Even Nazi hooligans
swear decorously in Germany, with no need of the 'fucks' and
'cunts' an English drunk needs to get through a sentence.

'So,' says Werner, when he has stared each of us down.
'The English Vikings. The folk dancers. You have no chance
against us. It would have been better if you had stayed at
home.'

'Maybe,' says Jamie. 'But we are here to win. At the tournament.'

'You don't eat meat?' says Werner, who eyes Jamie's salad
with some distaste. 'How can you fight?'

'I work on speed. Not strength,' says Jamie. 'And I am a
swordsman, not a . . .'

Werner's hand scythes through the air. His giant fist would have rearranged Jamie's handsome face permanently if he hadn't effortlessly leaned out of the way.

'Perhaps you are a swordsman,' says Werner, no hint of admiration in his voice. 'And perhaps I am just too drunk!' His belly laugh rattles the ashtray on the table. It would be churlish not to join in – and probably suicidal – so we manage some chuckles. Actually, I like him, which is a bit worrying.

'We know all about Stefan,' he tells us before taking another gulp of beer. 'But we don't know who *you* are. Or why you are interested in us.'

Sasha starts to speak, but Werner is staring at me. He holds up his hand. 'No. You tell me,' he says to me, having decided that I am the weakest link in the chain.

There is a theory that telling the truth is the best way of lying. This looks like the moment to test it out. 'It started last year,' I tell him. 'We received a threat. "Beware of the Dungeonmaster's Apprentice." It was probably from Richard Ambrose.'

Werner's eyes flicker. He does indeed know Richard.

'Richard or one of his underlings – maybe Alice Hathaway-Turner – crucified a cat on our door. Once you get death threats you have to investigate them,' I say.

Werner barks a short laugh right into my face. Deservedly so. 'Scheisse! If you know Richard you must be degenerates! Perverts! But you are right in one respect. I have been called the Dungeonmaster's Apprentice by some of our English friends. If you are lucky you will never find out the reason for this title.' His smile is as cheery as a dawn dip in a Norwegian fjord. I don't even like the sort of arguments that usually break out over Scrabble. I really must be somewhere else when the Dungeonmaster and Werner get out their toys.

'But I am really the sergeant-at-arms,' says Werner, nodding grimly to try to give us some idea of his own ferocity. 'I am in charge of discipline.'

He shows us some pointed yellow fangs in a ghastly smile then takes a long draught from his two-litre-glass boot of beer. 'But whatever I am, the Dungeonmaster is the leader. We follow him. Without question. And every winter we meet for the tournament. If you prove your worth you may even be invited to see the lakeside sacrifice.'

'This is a Viking sacrifice, right?' says Sasha, the school swot. 'In midwinter?'

'Precisely!' says Werner. 'It was an honour.' He laughs at the look on our faces. 'Odin's victims are always afforded a ritual hanging.'

'Afforded?' says Sasha.

'Afforded is the correct English usage,' says Werner. 'Perhaps you Americans should learn how to speak English.'

I couldn't help smiling, then yelping out loud as a sharp pain in my ankle reminds me of who pays my wages.

Werner waits for me to take some retaliatory action but then shakes his head in sorrow. 'In midwinter it was customary to sacrifice nine different animals. Including humans,' he continues. 'It was a way of honouring the courage of our enemies. This is why we have chosen the noose as our symbol. Ritual sacrifice has such important consequences for all those involved.'

'We will be stronger next time around?' I ask.

Something amusing occurs to him. His great belly starts to shake.

'Well,' he says, 'you could hardly be weaker. Could you?'

It's hard to keep up a gale of laughter on your own, usually, but Werner is having no difficulty. He eventually pauses to wipe his eyes but then one look at the new recruits and he is off again. The hilarity concludes with a thump of the table and the draining of his glass. 'I will arrange passes for the winter tournament! You will be here tomorrow at the same time. And if you wish to have any chance in the tournament I advise you to do some training. Only the strong survive!' With one more belly laugh he is on his way. And so are we. The troops are hungry, but this is not the place to ask for grilled tofu.

The next day sees Sasha at the wheel of our London taxi while I spread myself out on the back seat. Stefan will be driving the others in some bulletproof Volkswagen camper van. There is ample beer and Slivovitz on board, even enough for Jake. The wet-brains are already on their way, singing a rousing warrior song as they go. A peal of bells catches me just as I was enjoying the silence left by their exit.

'We could cut the bells down on our way out,' I tell Sasha as they toll merrily on.

'It's a tape,' she says. 'Or a CD. Didn't you know?'

'You're kidding. Let's put one of ours on. Give me something really radical.'

Sasha rummages in her pack for a while and finally locates a John Zorn CD. It's his 'Kristallnacht' piece, which features pounding drums, screeching violins, a lot of broken glass and speeches from Adolf Hitler. There are some harsh, abrasive passages too. And it should be played loud. At a Munich performance I once attended, it was made clear that the paying customers would not be allowed out once the music had started. Perhaps Mr Zorn had grown weary of playing at a retreating audience. But he couldn't stop me falling asleep, being blind drunk after an earlier showing of the vastly superior *Wayne's World*. 'Kristallnacht' is good stuff though, refreshingly tart and bracing. You could probably use it to scrape barnacles off the bottom of ships. And it sounds really good broadcast through a bell tower at the surrounding countryside. I bet the RAF didn't do as much damage as this. The immediate effect is some seriously demoralised farmyard animals. The chicks are clucking, the cows are mooing – and speaking of cows, here comes the nasty old bag from the farm opposite.

'Kruzifixe!' she says. I never liked people saying that. As if there aren't already enough crucifixes littered about Bavaria. They're everywhere, hanging off pub walls, round people's necks, even ruining the noble art of swearing. The enraged woman says it over and over again. 'Kruzifixe! Kruzifixe!'

As more peasants appear, one of them jabs the air with a pitchfork.

Viking curses were once sent by large poles pointed in the direction of the recipient. A horse's head would often be mounted on the end of these "niding poles" to help project the force of Hela, goddess of death. Sasha wears a horse's skull ring on the middle finger of her right hand, often referring to this finger as an "organic niding pole". Not that she needs any help in casting curses. By the time she's given the peasants a good jabbing with this digit they stay well and truly cursed. They cross themselves as Sasha steps on the gas.

'I think you frightened them,' she says. 'Glowering like that.'

'It's you. You witch.'

'It was the music. That was so cool,' she says. 'Jewish noise. Rage music. Payback for the Holocaust. Blasting out of a German church. Did you know "Zorn" means "rage"?'

I picture John Zorn, the archetypal puny little nerd. His

all-consuming political rage might well have something to do with the suffering of his people over thousands of years. It might also have something to do with his slightness of stature, his weedy physique and his silly glasses.

'What's that fiendish laugh for?' asks Sasha.

'You'll never be able to play that CD again,' I tell her.

'Oh, yeah?' she says, but even Sasha wouldn't dare ask the enraged peasants for her CD back. I'm still smiling as the enraged villagers disappear from our rear mirror. Until I realise that we are driving to the Dungeonmaster's ice fortress. To almost certain death.

The Dungeonmaster lives somewhere near the Bavarian Alps, not too far from where a certain failed painter maintained a mountaintop retreat. I often think the world would have been a better place if they had let Hitler paint and me play the piano. But Sasha seems to like it this way around. She does like her adventures. Her eyes are sparkling as we meet the others at a service station two hours away from those bloody bells.

For some reason this facility is not full of people in replica football kits stuffing themselves full of hamburgers from plastic boxes. The calm and prosperous locals seem to think that reasonably priced, high-quality food should be on sale to the general public. There is, however, one person demonstrating *le style anglais:* Jake, who has crashed out on the table, snoring drunkenly. As we join them Jamie is quizzing Stefan about the Dungeonmaster.

'Why is he allowed to hold a neo-Nazi festival every year?'

'It is a gathering of nationalists,' says Stefan firmly. 'And in any case he comes from a very respected family. A dynasty. He has been very clever about organising his resources. His army is called a sports training club. He even gets a grant from the council to maintain his fortress.'

'And they're cutting grants to artists!' says Sasha. Which is certainly keeping me awake at nights.

There is then some excited chatter about the execution methods employed by the Vikings, which I'm hoping not to experience, although the Dungeonmaster may have other views. One of them involved pulling out the lungs and stretching them over the ribcage, a death as long and drawn out as listening to Jake explaining endlessly that he isn't a drunk: he just 'likes a drink'.

The more I listen to this bloodthirsty banter the more I want to hitch a lift back to London. But someone has to look after Sasha. Who is looking a little pie-eyed on her new double dose of Prozac. Unfortunately she feels even less like eating as a result. Any more of this and she will be bony enough to get modelling work.

An hour later both of our vehicles have arrived at the private track that leads to the Dungeonmaster's fortress, a circular red-brick building that was built by the Nazis with slave labour. There are already scores of heavy trucks parked in the distance. Cloddish music wafts towards us, along with a heavy odour of beer, sausages and human waste. Any self-respecting pig would turn its nose up at such an affront to the senses; you almost expect to see rock fans queuing up to buy tickets.

At the gates is a scowling skinhead in grubby combats propping a bottle of beer on one of the best-maintained beer guts I have ever seen. It's as if he is trying to store a lifetime's supply in his stomach, just in case Bavaria goes Muslim.

'Can't wait to try some of that lager!' says Jake.

'We stay sober until the tournament!' Sasha tells him.

'Beer is liquid bread,' says Stefan.

'Absolutely!' says Jamie, who is also fond of the fluid grain. 'The blood of the hop. The fifth element!'

'The fifth element is ice!' chides Sasha. 'Ice is very important in German magic.'

'It's very important in a gin and tonic,' says Jamie irrefutably.

And there's another of Sasha's smiles. Just for Jamie. I really must see if I can arrange for him to walk into some friendly fire, once the bullets start flying.

The skinhead barks something into a walkie-talkie. Shortly after, an old army van drives up from the fortress. Werner leaps out and addresses the skinhead in Bavarian, using the intimate form of 'you'.

'You! You fat arsehole. Don't you ever stop swilling ale and stuffing yourself?'

'Werner! You swine!'

Werner starts sparring with the guard, a common form of greeting among manly Bavarians. When they have completed ritually poking and prodding each other, the footsoldier pats his solid stomach. 'That's prosperity, you fool!' The lads share a big grin and a big bear hug. Although some tiresome shrinks would insist that there is homo-eroticism buried somewhere in this ghastly coupling, there is certainly none for the observer, just the sight of wobbly stomachs and unshaven jowls rubbing together.

'We have some English comrades to join us,' quoths Werner, his voice booming with beer and bonhomie. He notices Sasha's cool stare. 'And an American, of course.'

The skinhead looks Sasha over but sees nothing he wants. Not enough meat probably. Then he scrutinises each of the men long enough to form an opinion of our possible fighting ability. After that he gives us an almost imperceptible nod to welcome us to the Dungeonmaster's domain.

We park among a strange mixture of top-of-the-range Audis and Mercs and rusted tin from the Eastern bloc. Sasha excites some lecherous dribbling from the oafs sat around long trestle tables piled high with food and beer. There are whole roast chickens, every single type of potato known to man, pretzels, enormous salads, and plates of radishes shaved thinly and sculpted into intricate origami patterns. It's noisy outside what with the medieval soldiers practising for the tournament and the Hell's Angels revving up their motorcycles. The inside of the fortress is a sonic holocaust. Our boots clatter along high echoey corridors past a number of rehearsal rooms full of Black Metal bands. Apart from the endless din of men drinking and fighting and the bands rehearsing, it also has to be said that some predominantly masculine environments could be a little more fragrant. I'm only thinking of Stephanie, you understand. It's a shame to subject such a delicious creature to such brutish unpleasantness. And I do hope she will show up again soon. I've seen quite enough of her crude brother Stefan.

Each dormitory appears to be a bubbling cauldron of beer, fags, sweat and testosterone, although Sasha and I have a room to ourselves. When we have each claimed our space we are led into a medieval kitchen lit by a roaring fire. Soon we are seated around a long banqueting table where Werner offers us hot spicy wine or beer.

'We don't drink,' says Sasha, and I'm glad she has taken on the responsibility of uttering such heresy.

'Persons with a genuine medical condition may be excused the communal banqueting hall, but only after basic training. If you join us you will have to drink. Mead is holy in our religion. We brew our own. It is blessed by our priestesses, so it can only do you good. Come now. Precisely five litres of good German beer a day promotes long life, health and happiness.'

'I'm an alcoholic,' I tell him.

'Jewish nonsense. Like psychoanalysis. We will teach you to drink in moderation. Like us.'

There is a great roar at this and the drinking horns are raised as one as a big blonde woman with a serious cleavage and china-blue eyes comes to the aid of the thirst-stricken. She is wearing a low-cut plain dress and a tight leather bodice on which the Odin's Knot symbol is displayed. I steel myself for some impenetrable local dialect but she's a Londoner. 'Come on, darling. Drink up. I know you want to.'

I can almost hear the voice of Richard Ambrose and other male sexual predators: 'Come on! You know you want it!' This time it's different though. I really am gagging for it. Even without the pussycat smile. And the warm moist cleavage. But just as those insistent white globes draw closer, Werner puts his arm around my shoulder, enveloping me in a fog of sweat, lager and leather.

'Drink slowly. With the comrades. We will overcome your problem.'

Someone claps me on the back as a bone drinking horn full of foaming wheat beer is placed in my hand. I look over at Sasha. She gives me a resigned smile. When in Rome do as the Romans do. And when in Valhalla . . .

The first few inches of the thick, cold brew are a struggle but I drink on anyway as the throng bang the table with their fists. I feel a great rush of pleasure and excitement as soon as the golden fluid kisses the lining of my stomach. And once it's rampaged through my veins and found the long-dormant pleasure zone in my brain there is nothing to do except laugh out loud. Werner, who is not so bad really, obviously shares my exhilaration.

'More beer here!' he calls. 'Warriors need to drink!' he says, and never was a truer word spoken. 'Besides, if you don't drink how can you sing?' asks Werner, starting to bang the table with the others as they start to sing. Even me.

The words aren't so important as long as you put a bit of feeling into them. And Sasha looks twice as desirable. I can see a bright full moon through the window. And it is a simple matter to channel those gleaming silver moonbeams directly through my own polished skull as I grasp another drinking horn firmly and raise it to my lips. The party continues, more or less the same one the Vikings might have had. There are endless toasts and party tricks. Joshing and boasting.

Anything that can be contested is: beer-drinking, arm-wrestling, shouting, singing, knife-throwing, axe-hurling – even knocking nails into a barrel with the thin end of a hammer. I don't know about you, but it beats sipping wine while discussing the ins and outs of the British Labour Party. And there is going to be more to chew on than tofu and water chestnuts. An entire roast pig arrives, at one point, sometime after the first gallon of ale has been consumed. There's a cocktail too: raw instant coffee on a slice of lemon over Slivovitz. Bite down on the coffee and lemon, then pour the plum brandy through the wreckage. It's vital. Refreshing. And you don't tend to miss those brain cells once they're gone. It might have been this drink that inspired me to take Sasha's beret off and instigate a few rounds of 'Beret'. After the first few throws the game spreads like wildfire; soon the air is full of baseball caps, fur balaclavas and even a Viking helmet. There is an outbreak of beaming smiles and table-thumping. It takes some time for the level of drunken buffoonery to subside, but when it does it is only to make way for a face-pulling competition. There is a British folk pastime known as girning, usually involving a toothless old man sticking his face through a horse-collar and pulling a face. The teenage Satanists on the next table are taking it in turns to mount the table, hold their drinking horns aloft and then snarl demonically at their comrades. Their black blood-spattered T-shirts hang off their skinny little bodies, each one as white as a button mushroom. Spots are being worn crimson this year – drops of bright fresh blood on the virgin-white snow of their faces.

'Hey! Crowley!' one of them shouts.

'They're talking to you,' says Sasha. Unfortunately scowling just makes me look even more like the old fraud. We order some food, which arrives just when we have drunk enough to contemplate dancing on the tables.

'Guad'n,' grunts Werner as we tuck in. This is Bavarian for 'good appetite' or 'Guten Appetit'. As usual it is accompanied by the lighting of a cigarette. Even though I don't dare say anything he reads my face easily enough.

'I'm so sorry,' he says, his tone implying the exact opposite. 'May I smoke? Perhaps our English guest will be able to tell us why English is the only language in which no one says good appetite. Or bon appetit,' he says, nodding at the French contingent. He is trying to imply we are barbarians who live on fish and chips – an impression Jake has done nothing to dispel.

'At least we managed to give the world a language people actually want to speak,' I say – about two hours later when Sasha and I are safely tucked up on the top floor.

'First time I've seen you smile in ages,' Sasha says, hopelessly drunk herself.

'This is great,' I tell her. 'I think I've found my inner hooligan.'

'Well, make sure you don't lose him. We have to get enough evidence to stop the Dungeonmaster. The world must know about what's going on here.'

And the world must know that Sasha Kristinson found it first. But I'm too happy to argue.

10

WHAT GOES UP must come down. But the Fourth Reich does not recognise hangovers. One bottle of beer with your breakfast and you do the morning drill. Then a routemarch with full pack. It's not negotiable. Our host is Werner, a man with limited patience for those who can't manage a hundred press-ups. The afternoon is devoted to weapons: swords, staves, guns and knives. Also competitive drinking, the only sport at which Jake can hope to compete. After a week of this we are fit, but no nearer meeting the Dungeon-master than we were in London. 'You must complete the training!' says Werner. But will we die in the attempt?

Considering the amount of beer this army consumes, it's a miracle the collateral damage isn't a lot higher than it actually is, with a mere handful of the troops carted off to have their bones knitted back together. But the most dangerous weapon of all remains Sasha's sharp tongue. She is such a spiteful little madam. Always able to find those tender places with the tip of her crop. So when she calls a dawn conference in our room the day before Xmas we are all there. Except for Stefan, who has been busy with old friends since we arrived.

'The Dungeonmaster has a well-guarded hide-out, half-way up the Virgin's Blush,' she informs us, pointing out the spot on the map.

'What?'

'It's that mountain with the forest on it. You can see it from here.'

'How did you find that out?' I ask.

'That's need-to-know, soldier,' says Sasha.

'You've shagged someone.'

'I wouldn't betray *you*,' she says. 'I just pretended I was interested in what some guy said. Story of my life, really.'

Once we have made it to the foot of the Virgin's Blush it is time to break open the beer. It is nine a.m. and Jake is thirsty. And while Sasha is off relieving herself behind a tree we dip into Jake's speed. What with that and occasional nips from Jamie's whisky, the long upward tramp presents few problems. Except for Jamie's comprehensive update from the world of alternative morris dancing.

'What is morris dancing?' says Sasha after a while.

'It's a fertility dance. To English roots music,' I tell her. Just don't say 'folk'. It's unacceptable these days. Although homophobic rappers are guaranteed a respectful profile in any broadsheet. As long as they're American, of course. Our own imbeciles just won't do.

'We're the best mixed side in south London,' Jamie says in response to no one's enquiry.

'Mixed?' asks Sasha.

'Men and women. And a pre-operative transsexual. Esmeralda.'

So he's still at it. Sorry. She's still at it. Five years of female hormones and she could still terrify most scrum halves.

'Doesn't she have two sons?' I ask.

'They used to be sons. Who knows what they are now? And last week we trashed the Morden Morris Men. We fucked them right off. Sent 'em home with their tails between their legs.'

Well, it makes about as much sense as Sasha's never-ending fight with her father. At least the Morden Morris Men are still alive – although those three-foot-long beards leave this open to question.

There may be those who would find a long walk up a densely forested snow-capped mountain interesting. While the air is fresh and zestful and we are adequately supplied with tall trees and small squirrels, there is a noticeable lack of comfortable sofas or freshly brewed coffee. Although someone has gone to the trouble of erecting a vividly painted crucifix, perhaps as a reminder that some fates are worse than a nature ramble with Jake.

By eleven o'clock Sasha finally heeds our mutinous mutterings and lets us find some trees to sprawl against.

'The metal lads from Norway say the dungeonmaster's a fat bastard these days,' says Jake.

He takes a swig from a big bottle of German whisky, a brew rough enough to make even his eyes water.

'Keep it under your hat, but I heard he might be mutating into a woman,' says Jamie.

'Mutating?' says Sasha.

'Sorry. But he may be taking hormones. And you know what happens to some transsexuals. They end up in strange no man's land. Between the sexes. We could be facing the most dreaded of all opponents: a fat, angry lesbian.'

Anyone else would have got a lecture at this point, but our leader stays silent. Perhaps it's because she fancies him and perhaps it's because he's armed with a spiked metal ball on a big stick. It seems to be difficult for him to negotiate even polite conversation without a weapon in his hand.

'What's that?' asks Sasha.

'It's a nobbler,' he says. 'One biff with this and you stay nobbled. I want to crush the Dungeonmaster's skull with it.'

'Isn't Werner always with him?' I ask.

'In theory. But there's always chances when the fighting gets messy. When a line fight degenerates into a melee.'

'This isn't that re-enactment bollocks,' says Jake. 'This is going to be a ruck.'

'Call it what you will,' says Jamie, flexing his nobbler. 'The result is the same. The spilling of blood. The banging of heads. And a good time had by all.'

Although Sasha is keen to continue on upwards to where certain death awaits, the chaps are in a talkative mood, especially as the whisky and speed circulate once more. I'm keen to encourage them because the more time we spend reminiscing the less time we might spend being flayed alive further up the mountain.

From where we sit we can just about see the fortress and the crowd clustered around the stage where the bands are performing. This has inspired the lads to spend about half an hour rubbishing the once-famous rock stars I used to accompany – quite rightly. When I attempt to excuse myself by mentioning my jazz and classical CV, the lads almost retch up their beer in disgust. 'Middle-class shite!' says Jake. Which for him sums up the few thousand years of music before the Clash.

I am then reduced to mentioning my touring days with Jimmy Witherspoon – the sort of blues legend that Clapton and all the others look up to. Needless to say, Jake and Jamie haven't heard of him, while both being blues fans.

'You don't look like a bluesman,' says Jamie.

'Some might think the interesting thing about music is what it sounds like,' I say. 'Not what it looks like.' But some might be in a very small minority indeed. Audiences tend to listen with their eyes.

'The Witherspoon tour went all over Europe,' I tell them as their eyes wander and they start to fidget. 'Big audiences. Went down a storm. The one review I saw, written by a white man called Jeremy, said that it was a disgrace that Jimmy Witherspoon should be backed by white musicians. The audience was of course entirely white, as it always is for the blues.'

'So what are you saying?' says Sasha. 'Show business sucks? We know. Why does it matter?'

It's a good point. One I can't answer.

'I might have known you'd be into jazz!' says Jake. 'Middle-class shite!' He may not be aware he has already used this. There is very little whisky left. He stands up to deliver a long speech about punk being the only true rock and roll. And he thinks *I'm* living in the past.

' . . . one of the Clash has to drive a cab now.'

As he always should have done. But there's no space to say it as Jake lets out a great endless blurt of pig-ignorance.

' . . . punk was the last genuine working-class movement in this country,' he says eventually.

'Really? I thought it was Thatcherism.'

'Fuck off. You were probably just a student. At least punk flushed all the fucking students down the pan. No more shite like Genesis.'

'I always hated them. But the only punk star I knew was called Timothy.'

'Timothy?' spits out Jake. 'Who the fuck was that?'

'T.V. Smith. An excellent man. Very sharp, very funny. But his real name is Timothy.'

'Wow! You knew T.V. Smith.'

'Yes. His real name's Timothy.'

Even Sasha is aware that this is not an immediate signifier of working-class credibility. As if watching *Who Wants to be a Millionaire?* three times a week was anything to aspire to.

'What happened to Gaye Advert?' asks Sasha. 'She was hot.'

Dark alluring Gaye and her big black eyes. So different from the Benny Hill dolly birds who used to giggle and simper in the days before punk. Just before that pumpkin-faced misery Andrea Dworkin declared all sexual intercourse to be rape.

'That's just about what I said to T.V. first time I met him,' I tell her. ' "What happened to Gaye Advert?" ' He didn't like that. You could tell that was what everyone asked him.'

'So what *did* happen to her?'

'She's his wife.'

'Did you meet her?'

'Yes. She's a lovely woman. Works for the council. Looks a bit New Age actually.'

'The council?' Sasha is shocked and disappointed. The haunted woman who 'looked through Gary Gilmore's eyes'? Say it ain't so!

'Housing department,' I say, gently but firmly. 'She never got over the shock of actually getting paid when you did some work. Someone else doesn't nick all the money. You get paid. But T.V. never lost the taste for singing his protest songs. He's still out there. Even a man who hasn't had a hit for a quarter of a century can still gig as a protest singer. Wearing a hole in his fretboard with the same four minor chords. Even that's more popular than jazz.'

Sasha hears a different version of this last bit, as if she has installed software that automatically cuts out any whining about jazz.

'Gaye Advert,' she breathes, still lost in the magic of it all. Even though her heroine never became a junkie or committed suicide. Gaye is probably sat by the fireside right now waiting for her camomile tea to brew. While the woman she inspired is taking slugs from the communal whisky bottle and waiting for the speed to come around again. If I can just keep these stories going, and if the bottle keeps circulating, I might even get her to forget about the rest of this mission. Sasha's eyes are softening, Jake has been blurred since mid-morning and Jamie is dancing a jig while playing the tin whistle, looking like the leader of a progressive folk-rock band in about 1971. I may be wrong, but these troops may not strike dread into the hearts of Werner and his pals. Surely Sasha will have to call it off?

'I used to taunt T.V. with the theme tune to *Home and Away*,' I say. 'When we shared a hotel room on tour.'

'We belong together . . . ' starts Jake, arms above his head as he launches into it, full throttle. It takes a good verse or so before he realises he is singing alone. He's proving my point though. It's a proper song. And very hard to forget after the first hundred or so times.

'It seemed very well written to me,' I tell them, because it's the last thing they want to hear. There is a rising chorus of ominous muttering as I continue, but I'm helpless to stop, prodded on by speed and beer. 'It's got a few chord changes here and there, unlike your average protest song. It's quite uplifting.'

'Yeah. The beach on a sunny day. And teenage girls in swimming costumes,' says Sasha. Her voice is scathing but, yet again, she is talking about what music looks like, as people invariably do.

But it is time to change the subject. Or they may well throw me in the ice-cold river just behind us.

Jake and Jamie look a bit restless. We have been sat here far too long without a fight developing. They don't even need an excuse to start one, just standing up and stretching their legs at the same time seems to flow seamlessly into some energetic wrestling.

'This is fun, isn't it?' says Sasha, bathed in a great glow of whisky, beer, speed and Prozac. 'Go on, admit it. You're actually enjoying yourself. Back to nature. Near the end of our quest.'

Perhaps we finally have become the warrior and the wise woman – although this time around she's the brave warrior and I'm the haggard crone.

'The kids are getting a bit boisterous,' I say as the pace of the fight steps up a bit.

'You wouldn't want them to be girlsterous, would you?' says Sasha. 'They're our troops.'

And that's an excellent punch that has landed squarely on Jamie's chin. There's a short pause while he assesses the damage and then they are off again, grappling and cursing.

'It's nice seeing the kids playing,' I say.

'Yeah, Kiss me.'

Apparently it's good to kiss in front of your children. It sets a good example. Mummy and Daddy don't spend their entire lives arguing. But our embrace doesn't do anything to distract Jake and Jamie from their fight. The tussle may have started as a game, but the second time Jake lands a punch

Jamie pulls him into a backward roll and launches him into an impressive parabolic arc with the help of a two-footed push to his stomach.

Perhaps this knocked the breath out of him. There must be some reason why Jake makes no attempt to break his fall and lands squarely on his head in a shallow part of the stream. There is an ominous crack of bone as his head finds a most inconveniently placed boulder. And no cry of distress from Jake, who is lying in a most unnatural posture – his body on land and his head under water. It's the sort of posture you could fold a rag doll into, or a human being with a broken neck. It seems ironic that exposure to water seems to have killed him, a substance he spent most of his life avoiding – certainly for the purposes of washing or drinking.

While I had no time for Jake while he was alive, and he is going to be a bloody nuisance now he's dead, if I had 'accidentally' killed him I would probably try to look a bit concerned. Or say sorry or something. Nothing much shows in Jamie's face as he ambles over to take Jake's pulse.

'Is he dead?' I ask. Jamie nods briskly.

'I'm sorry. It's a bit of a shame. But he was going for it. I had to do something.'

I look at our leader. The last thing I expect to see is a big, beaming smile.

'It's the day of the sacrifice,' says Sasha, punching the air in triumph. 'We have sacrificed one of ours first. It means we will win! We will defeat the Dungeonmaster!'

More positive thinking courtesy of the Prozac corporation, no doubt. Or has she just gone mad again? Rather than attempt to answer that, I look at Jamie. Perhaps he will have something slightly less insane to contribute.

'It's quite handy, him landing like that,' he says, the first time I have heard the word 'handy' in this context. 'It will look like he has drowned. He just bashed his head while diving in.'

'Why would he dive into a freezing-cold river?' I ask.

'Because he was a drunken idiot.'

He's right, but a little dab of compassion might be in order. For form's sake. Especially when you've just killed a chap.

Sasha's not much better, eyes shining with joy. 'It's given me a great idea! We can kill the Dungeonmaster and make it look like an accident! Stage some duel or something! Jake hasn't died in vain. That is his gift to us. That is his legacy.'

Her eyes are shining in the clear grey light. I don't know exactly what I'm supposed to say at this moment. But I can't find anything to match her euphoric mood. She has often told me to think positively. She may even be right. But this is ridiculous.

'Isn't there some Zen story about a meditation teacher who hit his pupils' heads with a big stick?' says Sasha. 'If they ever lost their posture or stopped concentrating, the teacher crept up behind them and whacked them on the head. Then he killed one of them.'

'Which was "a bit of a shame",' I say to Jamie. But he doesn't seem to notice.

'That year they had an unusually high number of enlightened pupils,' says Sasha.

'There you are, then,' says Jamie. 'It is our task to put this unfortunate incident behind us and proceed onwards. The wise warrior doesn't dwell in the past.'

This from a man who spends most of his leisure time recreating medieval battles. 'We should mark his passing though. Perhaps we could have a short wake,' he says, flourishing his tin whistle ominously.

'You remember people every day,' says Sasha. 'They live inside your head. Funerals are always flawed.'

'Yeah,' I say. 'At my dad's there was a gravediggers' strike. But that's Liverpool for you. We had to drive an hour out of the city, at the speed hearses drive, to find somewhere that actually could do a funeral.'

'Lots of people?' says Sasha.

'It was a good turnout, but there was a much bigger procession down Streatham High Street for one of the train robbers.'

'The flower seller?' says Sasha. 'I remember that. Yeah, well, he was royalty round there, I suppose. You promised to take me to those Elvis restaurants once.'

And she's still trying to make me feel guilty about it, even as we stand next to a fresh cadaver. Who could forget the two competing Elvis impersonators – one Italian, one Greek – both refusing to give up their nightly performance as the King in adjoining restaurants? It might be worth a smile in any other circumstances.

'Well, I'm going to send Jamie on his way,' says Sasha as if there was some argument about it. She kneels down and scoops some of the flowing water over his body, cooing what sounds like a lullaby as she does so, using one of the ancient magical languages I was too lazy to learn. If only she had some soap it would be the first decent wash he has had in decades, but maybe she is speeding the passage of his soul to its next manifestation. I wonder whether he will be spending so much energy fighting a losing battle next time around. Jamie's whistle pipes on, simultaneously a dirge-like lament and a piercing irritant.

'Shall we call it off, then?' I say.

'No!' says Sasha, scowling. 'We will ride the energy Jake

has released! We are going to win! Today we will confront the Dungeonmaster! We will do it for Jake!'

Jamie thinks that's a better idea than I do. So he takes Sasha's arm and strides off. They do make a nice couple. A brave soldier and his fair maiden. It seems odd that they haven't done the deed yet. But then she'd tell me. Wouldn't she?

I have a passport and credit card in my leather jacket. If I don't go back to the fortress I'm going to lose my copy of Shakespeare's sonnets on mini-disk and a few shirts. I might miss the final assault on the Dungeonmaster, but I should be able to get over that. I really don't have to follow them if I don't want to. But there's nothing much waiting for me without Sasha. Just whatever's claimed Jake. I take one last look at his body as the water washes over him. 'And nothing stands except for his scythe to mow,' say the sonnets, with reference to time. I suppose Sasha would find that line unacceptably English and defeatist. But even she can't defeat grumpy old Kronos, the lord of time. She might be able to kick him in the shins first, but the end result will be the same. Death. The void. Nothing. Nada. Nowt, as we used to say up north.

As we get further up the mountain the walk becomes as sombre as a family Sunday: long periods of silent resentment, muttered curses and the occasional outburst of murderous rage and spite – although the other two handle it a good deal better.

'I keep on wondering whether it was an accident,' says Sasha, two backbreaking hours later. Jamie looks down at Sasha. His eyes are untroubled by guilt; he is merely faintly amused that we are being so girlie about a spot of spoilage. Wear and tear.

'It's a setback, admittedly,' says Jamie.

'A setback?' begins Sasha until Jamie cuts her off.

'If Jake was unfit to fight, it's better that we know it now.'

'Kiss my ass,' says Sasha.

Jamie's eyes twinkle, but then he decides not to share whatever witticism has just occurred to him. Sasha looks very angry. And she is armed. She has Kate's gun trained on Jamie.

'Now don't be a silly girl. These things happen.'

'And you've killed him. And you're just standing there like nothing happened.'

Jamie looks puzzled for a moment then sees a way out. 'It won't help if I burst into tears. Or stand there feeling sorry for myself. Moaning on all day and not being any bloody use.'

For some reason Sasha looks at me. And in the instant she does so Jamie steps forward and disarms her. He makes it look easy, but I suspect most other people would be dead by now. She looked mad enough to shoot him a moment ago, but he never looked remotely afraid. The idea that he might not be invincible doesn't seem to cross his mind. As he opens her weapon and sees that it is loaded he does look a bit cross for once. But it's over in the time it takes for your new computer to become obsolete.

'The safety was off! You could have killed me! I should put you across my knee and give you a good spanking for that, my girl.'

'You would never touch me unless I let you.'

Jamie mimes a yawn. 'Depends if you've just tried to kill me or not. On active service discipline is sometimes required.'

'You're working for me. What's the penalty for killing a quarter of our army?'

'You've got to allow for breakages,' he says.

Sasha and I look at each other. Then we look at him for a while. He's quite happy to return our stares.

'If either of you had served your countries you would know there is no point in crying over spilled milk,' he says.

Before we can get any further with that a rustle in a nearby bush announces the arrival of Werner. His massive fist is wrapped around a revolver.

'I will take your weapons,' says Werner.

'No, you won't,' says Jamie.

'I will take your weapons.'

'Well, you can try, old boy. But you're going to come a cropper. Why don't we fight for it? Let me get my swords out. Anyone can wave a gun about. Let's settle this like gentlemen.'

I would have shot him, but Werner nods in agreement. As soon as Jamie produces a pair of weapons the two warriors actually stand there discussing sword-forging technique as Sasha and I sidle off to a safe vantage point. With a bit more judicious sidling we might be able to slink away to safety. But we might as well watch Jamie lay his life down for us. It's the least we can do.

'Are you sure you want to do this?' says Jamie. 'You won't win, you know. And it would be such a shame to die on Xmas Eve.'

Although there is six feet between them, they are both at the ready, heavy swords clutched with both hands, each looking for a moment's hesitation or weakness in the other. It's a solemn moment. But stealing a glance at Sasha, I can see her eyes sparkle. If he dies it will be mostly her fault. She hired him to do this. But she is feeling no anxiety or guilt, just exhilaration.

Werner is the first to move, rushing forwards with a mighty roar as if he is about to carve his initials on Jamie's face. Jamie launches his sword directly at him, propelled as fast as any arrow by the heel of his hand. It races through the three feet of air between them and buries itself up to the hilt in Werner's chest. Werner staggers backwards, clutching at the sword, but he isn't going to do anything about that or indeed anything else. A few seconds later he is watching the sky, flat on his back.

'Now that's what I call piercing,' says Jamie.

I'm still looking a bit goggle-eyed, I suppose. Jamie raises an eyebrow, posing the question: 'Well, what of it?'

'What happened to honour?' I ask him. 'The noble warrior? A fair fight?'

'If he can't get out of the way of a hurled missile he should pack it in.' There is the unmistakable sound of the death rattle, an evacuation of air from both ends. 'Well, he has packed it in. Never mind. Must get on.' He retrieves his sword, gives it a bit of a wipe then flourishes it over his head.

He is looking chipper. But then I suppose two kills in one morning would brighten anyone's day. I just want to go home. Except there is no home. And the wife's gone mad. Jamie may never have been sane and that just leaves me as the voice of moderation. But who is going to listen? Sasha is looking at Jamie with pure shining love in her eyes.

'Come on!' says Jamie, giving his sword a good brandishing. 'There's the Dungeonmaster to defeat. And no doubt a few fair maidens to rescue along the way.'

At that moment a black crow launches itself upwards from a nearby tree.

Sasha looks at me. 'It's Werner's spirit,' she says.

I suppose he could be off to some karmic waiting room or

other, whiling away the time before his next tour of duty. And Santa Claus might be bringing us all presents at midnight tonight. I start searching the forest for some clear sign that we should pack this in: three human skeletons tied together, perhaps, or a sign saying 'This is beyond a joke. Go home.' But there is nothing except a thicket of tall trees ahead. And somewhere in there the Dungeonmaster awaits.

'Shouldn't we bury him?' says Sasha. 'They'll find him.'

'He's biodegradable,' says Jamie. 'But we should definitely recycle his usable parts.'

He pats the body down, after which we share a few hundred Deutschmarks; Jamie keeps Werner's leather waistcoat. 'This is how most knights got their armour in the old days, you know,' says Jamie, chirpy as ever. 'It was far too expensive to buy brand-new.'

He whistles some folk ditty or other as he strides off uphill. Sasha scampers off after him. I can stand here waiting to be transported back in time before Sasha's mission to expose the Dungeonmaster started. Or I can follow them.

I eventually decide to follow, although not until after I have given the first option a great deal of thought. I can't change the habits of a lifetime. Tagging along with whoever might protect me made me the man I am today. And so we trudge on upwards, energised by the proximity of death, although some of us are wondering whether one gun between three people is really enough. Half an hour later Sasha's wake-up call arrives.

We hear the footsteps before we see who is following us, but by then we have been surrounded. Three skinheads with rifles and a team of beefy Nordic types with baseball bats argue in what sounds like Swedish, but it's not too hard to judge what they're going to do to us. As they close in, Jamie reaches for the gun but a baseball bat deadens his arm. I can only land one kick, which goes nowhere useful. And then a man with too many facial tattoos relieves me of the burden of consciousness.

11

SASHA AND I have been secured flat on our backs to a stone slab. There are heavy leather cuffs at our wrists and ankles. We can rattle our chains. But we aren't going anywhere. The itching turns out to be rough black blankets covering the lower halves of our naked bodies. We have been painted with the thirteenth rune, an ominous double-hook-shaped daub in thick smeary red over our hearts. Marked for death. A yuletide sacrifice a long way from home. Sasha has a big purple bruise on her forehead but appears to be breathing.

Stars are visible through a high window, but visibility is otherwise limited. Through the incense-laden murk it is just possible to make out hooded figures stood around a sacrificial altar on the other side of our cell.

The fixtures and fittings approximate to those of a night-club going for the dungeon aesthetic. But this appears to be the real thing. There is a rack of pincers and pliers to our left. Irons are being heated in a brazier to our right.

The room is lit by torches, and there is a strong smell of hashish. Above us is a large slowly rotating swastika painted in fluorescent green on a black backing. This is a variant on the age-old sunwheel symbol: three interlocking swastikas. I remember Sasha had some visualisation exercise involving the rotation of swastikas; you could either turn back time or speed it up, depending on whether they moved clockwise or anticlockwise. All you need to know about that is that she's always late. And that she managed to conjure up this reality in which we are to be this year's sacrificial victims.

The green symbol above us continues to move slowly anticlockwise, which I'm pretty sure Sasha said turns time backwards, if you want to have a go yourself. The Dungeonmaster certainly seems to be trying to move Europe a few thousand years back to a time when tribal warfare was more important than cultural exchange. But is he such a stickler for tradition that he would sacrifice human life? Then I recall that Jamie has just helpfully skewered one of his troops. Even the most indulgent host might look on this as a faux pas.

Some of the incense catches in my lungs and sets off a coughing fit that leaves me weak and teary-eyed. It also attracts the attention of a large man who waddles slowly towards us. His hood covers most of his fat face. A large ruby glitters on his middle finger. He also wears rings set with green and blue stones that no doubt have great occult significance. To the uninitiated these gaudy baubles signify only a tragic failure to understand the first rule of successful accessorising – less is more.

'You have come a long way to meet me,' he says in confident, unaccented English. He steps closer, into the light. And invites us to be awestruck. But the sight of a very fat man with random grey hair and a moon face pitted with savage craters is less than awesome. He is adequately sorted for chins and jowls, more than any reasonable person could ever need.

Eyebrows are being worn bushy and wayward this year – and grey. It really is best to remain invisible if you wish to preserve mystique. If this is the Dungeonmaster, he doesn't look very frightening at all. He looks like an absent-minded philosopher, which is more absent-minded than any scientist could ever be. He smells of cigarettes, menthol and eucalyptus. His clumps of greasy grey hair are as unruly as the Balkans, and as bleakly horrible, and also beyond any possible solution. There are patches of grey stubble distributed over what was intended to be a clean-shaven face. There is a more than adequate supply of black fur spouting from his ears. So he's rich and powerful. He has still broken the only universally agreed-on modern commandment: 'Thou shalt not be fat.' And old men with uneven grey stubble and luxurious growths of ear and nostril hair shouldn't really wander around dressed up as monks. It's not nice.

But it's him who has us tied up. As the irons heat up nicely.

'We left details of this place in London,' I tell him in a strange, croaky voice that doesn't seem to belong to me. 'Your secret is out.'

'There is no secret. And no one would miss you two. You're fugitives.'

We stare at each other for a while. When that's done it's clear there is no further purpose in trying to talk our way out of this or pleading for mercy.

'The twelve-limbed swastika,' he says, nodding upwards.

'The emblem of perfection. We used this after the war when our symbol was banned by the cowards, the appeasers. It is also set into the floor of Himmler's Wewelsburg Castle. In green marble. It was always my dream to re-create such a gateway for the forces of darkness here in Bavaria. While the rest of the world bows to the Jewish vision of Hollywood or the cruel, primitive ignorance of Africa, I will leave a monument to the ice-hard clarity of the north. Clear thinking. Ruthless action. Duty. Sacrifice. Honour.'

He sounds and looks terrifying. But he smells of embrocation and booze – eucalyptus, menthol and a waft of alcohol. It's an old codger's smell. And he is far too fond of raising his big bushy eyebrows for emphasis. But who will tell him?

'You have desecrated your bodies. And you thought you would pass as Aryan activists. How could perverts be committed to the creation of a new moral order? This King Alfred you have nailed through your penis . . . ' He waves a dismissive hand. I wait to see if he is joking. He isn't.

'It's a Prince Albert,' I say, pedantic to the last. 'It feels good.'

'It is degenerate! Sticking metal through your penis! How foolish! It is your *muscles* which must become cold steel! Your *will* must be as hard as iron! Why do you ape the practices of primitive people?'

'Couldn't you say that war is a bit . . . you know . . . primitive?' I say, talking very quietly now.

'Not at all. War is man's destiny. And it is only recently that we have forgotten our duty. War is the answer to the most pressing question faced by modern man.'

'Yes,' I say. 'How do we get away from our wives and children?' This is said with feeling, but luckily Sasha is still unconscious. Annoying the Dungeonmaster is one thing, but it's quite another to tangle with the Supreme Ogress.

'There is no need to be trivial,' he says. 'You are courageous or you would not be here. You have not settled for an easy life.'

Just give me the chance, mate. Show me the couch and I'll lie on it.

'Where's Jamie? And Stefan?'

'Stefan will be taking part in your transformation. He is one of us. Jamie will fight for his life against another one of our prisoners. He is a warrior and therefore accorded respect. If he survives he can go. Meanwhile you can watch the tournament. And prepare yourself for death.'

With that he waddles off. There is a muttered conference with the hooded ghouls at the other end of the dungeon. As they leave, one of them turns and draws his finger swiftly across his throat.

While Sasha was unconscious I felt only love and pity for her. Now she's awake I want to do as much damage as possible. For this is all her fault.

'They've got Jamie,' I tell her. 'And Stefan always was on their side.'

'Jamie will rescue us,' says Sasha.

Good to know. For a moment I thought we were in trouble.

'Yeah,' I say. 'Maybe he can give you the sort of life you need. The adventures. The dicing with death. I've had enough.'

'You don't mean that,' she says.

Well, that's settled then. I thought I had said something that might possibly require a reply. Apparently not.

'This *would* happen just before my period,' she says. 'I feel terrible. And I've lost my Prozac. I feel really weird.'

I thought the foundations were trembling. And is that the rumble of distant thunder? Anything can happen in the days just before the flow of the sacred blood. And that's before her double dose of Prozac has been removed.

'We'll definitely go to America,' says Sasha, still playing with possible futures. 'See my mom before she dies.'

'It's too risky. And I'm sick of America.'

I'm probably just sick of short female Americans. But this isn't the right time to say that.

'You're just jealous. We're more successful than you.'

'There are just more of you! Anything produced in America can be marketed to more people! That's it!'

'You guys *need* America. To kick you up the ass. And you need me . . . to motivate you. I made you what you are today. I taught you everything. Group sex. The full-body orgasm.'

And how to get killed. But the rest is still true. She gave me the secret of eternal life – the Tantric technique of sperm-less orgasm. It's just using a small pelvic muscle to trap sperm inside the body during orgasm. It produces an intense longer-lasting orgasm. You can learn it in a week. But most blokes aren't interested. They'd rather watch the football. Or fight. Or drink.

'Remember that press agency guy telling you that your Tantric sex article was great?' I ask Sasha. ' "We could do with more of this women's interest stuff." '

'Yeah,' she says wearily. 'It's a shame men can only get excited by football, fighting and cars. And big tits.' She almost spits the last two words out, perhaps because she is boyish rather than bountiful. Then an impish smile appears on her pale lovely face. 'I don't know why you hate football and football fans so much,' she says. 'You're just like them.'

'What?' That's the most audacious thing she's ever said. It's grounds for divorce. From each and every one of our marriages.

'Don't look like that. Some football fans cling on to knowing obscure facts about football,' says Sasha. 'Like all this pointless stuff you know about music. And some of them support teams they know to be useless year after year. Just as you cling on to jazz even though you hate it.'

I am gasping now. Rage has flooded every single part of my body.

'Don't you ever . . . ever . . . ever say such a thing ever again!'

'Why not? You're just a closet football fan who won't own up to your own male obsessiveness.'

That does it. If we do get off this slab the first thing I'm going to do is wring her neck.

'It's not "obsessive" to know that Bill Evans is better than the Spice Girls,' I tell her, almost choking on my own words.

'I suppose you're always so angry because men can't create anything.'

'What?'

'I mean babies.'

'Oh, *that*! I thought you meant something important. Look, it's us that makes babies. You lot just carry them around for a while.'

'Then feed them and nurture them. Let them suck at our big nurturing breasts.'

'That's what all this is about.' Occasionally I get this demand for a baby. As if that would automatically solve everything. 'You just want bigger tits. Believe me, it really isn't worth ruining the rest of your life just to fill those things up with milk.'

We share a rueful glance. There isn't going to be a rest of our lives. And we're finishing off this one with an argument. But not after a small television monitor mounted high on the wall flickers into life. Domestic peace has been restored. We can shut up and watch the telly. On the screen the Dungeonmaster is seated on the main stage. Below him are thirty or so combatants dressed in various medieval warriors' costumes arranged around a small circular space in which two men stand, swords at the ready.

'Well, at least we get to see the tournament.'

'Yeah. You should be happy now. Vegging out in front of a television.'

'Well, look where your Internet mania got us . . . If only you'd let us watch Seinfeld . . . '

'You're just a zombie. I live life to the full.'

Not for much longer, dear.

' . . . just a whinger. You don't *do* anything.'

Luckily the fight's started. All I have to *do* now is watch the screen.

Jamie has finally got his wish. He's starring in a movie about the Middle Ages. The camera's on him as he faces a big fat lunk who looks East European. They circle each other for a while, swords raised, a tight little smile on Jamie's face. The other guy looks frightened, knowing he is outclassed. I don't want it to be real. But when one of Jamie's thrusts get past the other guy's shield, thick red blood spurts out.

'Is that real?' says Sasha.

The man on the floor is twitching. The camera zooms in on a pair of bloodshot eyes as they glaze over. It might be the moment when the spirit leaves the body. It might be an actor trying not to blink. He looks very still. And remains so.

'Look!' says Sasha. 'They're playing beret!'

And so they are. Sections of the crowd are hurling their baseball caps at each other. At least we will have left something behind us.

'Happy ending for Jamie,' says Sasha.

'Is it? Can they really afford to let him go?'

'Look. That was probably fake. This is just an initiation ceremony,' says Sasha.

'It *is* an initiation ceremony,' I tell her. 'Into the next life.'

Something flickers inside Sasha's eyes. She stares at me long enough to make sure I am ready to receive something of vital importance. 'Every day is an initiation ceremony,' she says, giving each word its full weight. 'Into this life. And into every other.'

It might have been comforting – in London over a mug of decaff. But this isn't the right place. Stranded on this stone shore. Waiting for the tide to wash us away.

'Tell me a story,' says Sasha, sounding surprisingly childlike.

I feel tired and trapped, all too aware that I'm doing something I don't want to, as the clock is ticking faster and faster and my time is running out. It's a familiar feeling for any father my age reading a bedtime story. But daddies have those heart-squeezing smiles to keep them going, just as I do with Sasha.

'A guy dies and goes to hell,' I tell her. 'He's rather surprised at how civilised everything is. Whatever you want you can have. There's champagne and Marmite toast for breakfast.' Sasha nods her approval. Her favourites. 'Then you can have a long walk in the countryside or a swim in the sea. There's tofu and water chestnuts for lunch. Afternoon theatre in the park in New York. The galleries are packed. Performance artists are rich and famous.' It's risky saying that as some of Sasha's old buddies did become famous. But she lets it pass.

'Is the devil English?' she says, smiling at me for some reason.

'The Devil is an English gentleman,' I say.

'The devil is a woman,' she replies.

Well, Camille Paglia says so anyway, the only other little terrorist who would be Sasha's equal if it came to a fight. Now *that* would be worth seeing. Female dwarf-wrestling, both of them fierce little rams born under the fire sign of Aries. Although Sasha might be overawed by finally meeting her heroine. I can't think why. At least Sasha works in the sex industry; she doesn't just pussy around writing academic dissertations about it. And I really should try to move us closer to the punchline of this joke, which is already as late as the child we keep trying for.

'One day the devil takes the new arrival out for a walk. They walk through pleasant countryside – clear babbling brooks, verdant pastures, rolling hills. The guy keeps telling the Prince of Darkness that hell is the nicest place he's ever been to. The devil thanks him. 'That's what they all say,' he says. By the time they have finished their Cuban cigars they come across foul-smelling black smoke billowing out of a great gaping hole in the ground. The devil starts to shake his head, more in sorrow than in anger. The new arrival looks down into the hole and sees nasty little imps prodding naked bodies with sharp tridents. The sound of weeping and wailing is heart-rending. The guy looks at the devil and says, "Who *are* these people?" The devil just sighs and says, "They're Catholic. They insisted." '

'That's neat,' says Sasha, smiling in recognition. We have what her mother once referred to as a mixed marriage – she's Catholic, I'm Protestant. This may be the root of our many problems, although it's just as likely to be her mother's curse. For she is the real witch in the family. Sasha's just an amateur compared with her. But before we can get any further with that, the Dungeonmaster's face appears on the screen.

'Forty-five minutes,' he tells us. 'You are going to die.'

His voice is gentle and reasonable, as if he is telling us for our own good. Perhaps he is.

'You must put your lives in order,' he continues. 'Before you can move on.'

The screen goes blank. As it soon will on a more permanent basis.

'It's probably all fake,' says Sasha. 'You don't get to join the Black Order without being in fear of your life.'

But we're not trying to join it. Are we, dear? Least, I wasn't. Perhaps I joined it the day I met Sasha. ('You always blame someone else!' Yes, dear.) But she might be right. They could just be trying to scare us. It is a straw of hope to clutch at. And just as I reach out to grasp this thin slippery reed, the screen changes to a close-up of the operating table, where a bundle of shivering black fur is staked out on a stone pentacle. It could be a particularly grisly hospital drama, except that the figures clustered around the table are wearing black-hooded robes. It looks like a veterinary drama set in a monastery, which would be a guaranteed hit in predominantly Catholic Europe. But it doesn't look as if this black bundle is being cured of anything. Sasha is straining every muscle in her body trying to break out of her wrist and ankle cuffs. As the triple-chinned Dungeonmaster raises his arms above his head to lead the faithful in a chant that successfully defies our attempt to make out a word of it.

'I can't look,' says Sasha. 'How can they do this?'

Sasha has often simulated the rape and torture of woman for the purposes of art. Hollywood seems to do little else these days except stage meaningless killings for adolescents. But no director anywhere in the known universe would dare to show the smallest dumbest animal with even a thorn in its paw. Some forms of life are actually sacred, at least as far as the censors are concerned. Unfortunately, whoever is filming this is not looking for mainstream distribution.

The chanting gets louder and more insistent as the ceremonial knife is held up to the light. The faithful cry and gibber as the knife is pulled across the cat's throat. Blood flows into a silver chalice as the animal twitches fitfully. After some ham-fisted butchery the head is finally severed, then placed upright on an altar. A clumsy zoom brings us far too close to this grisly-looking object, then the screen goes blank. Sasha weeps for a while. When the tears dry up she attempts to put on a brave face. That's even more upsetting, but I have to pretend it isn't.

'The day we met you told me a joke,' she says. 'Then you were too drunk to finish it. Maybe today's the day to tell me the rest.'

Because we are about to die. But there's no point in dwelling on that.

'You mean Two Pickets to Tittsburg? It won't really be funny now, babe. Not now I'm sober.'

'If I'm going to die, I want to hear the punchline,' she insists.

'Why did you wait all this time?'

'I thought it would be really cute to remind you about it. When we were sixty or something.'

And we probably aren't going to be sixty. Not this time around. I take a deep breath. 'A guy goes to Grand Central Station to buy two tickets to Pittsburg. The problem is that the ticket-seller is a lovely blonde woman with enormous breasts who is wearing a low-cut dress. Every time he tries to say, "Two tickets to Pittsburgh" it comes out as "Two pickets to Tittsburgh." It happens over and over until he has his first drink in years to get over the embarrassment. He drinks until he loses his job, then his wife. Eventually he ends up on the street. Until a short sassy angelic-looking blonde woman comes along and rescues him.'

Sasha is beaming away now. It is sometimes easy to make your partner happy. You just have to compliment them occasionally. I can't think why I don't do it more often.

'Once she's put him back on his feet again, he decided it would be a really good idea to test his new-found sobriety by trying to order two tickets to Pittsburgh. So the guy gets up to the ticket window and it's the same well-stacked woman. She's even wearing a push-up bra. She's darkened the insides of her cleavage to make her breasts look bigger.'

Sasha's face solidifies into grey slate. A fierce warrior rune known as the helm of all-prevailing will appears briefly on her forehead. I really shouldn't have reminded her of that.

'The guy concentrates really hard on saying "Two tickets to Pittsburgh", although it's agonising that the woman is more attractive than ever. She's a little heavier with the years, but even more bouncy and beautiful. She smiles sympathetically. He says, very slowly and carefully, "Two tickets to Pittsburgh, please." He opens his eyes to find she is smiling at him. Just as he's really ecstatic that he's managed not to say the word "tits" she says, "And how would you like your change?" He says, "Nipples and dimes".'

Sasha laughs briefly, once. 'Not bad,' she says.

Oh, well. And we're still going to die.

The next time the Dungeonmaster arrives he is still in his robes but the hood is down. It must be dress-down day. He is drinking mulled red wine from a silver goblet with ornamental barbed wire wrapped around the handle. As a further refinement of torture he has selected a form of music that is particularly distressing to Sasha – thoughtful jazz produced by technically adept musicians. You can't look at it and you can't dance to it – what could be worse? Although some people do find this European ambient stuff relaxing and soothing. It's turning up everywhere now: orgies, art installations, the occasional funeral. Anywhere nerves need soothing. You know the sort of thing. Against a backwash of clattering Third World percussion, a plaintive flugelhorn grizzles on for a while before giving up at the sheer hopelessness of human existence. Some finger cymbals chime. Clouds float by to the sound of East European yogic chanting. About twenty minutes later a double bass may play one extremely pertinent and resonant note. Equally, the musician may have decided not to bother, having reached a state of Zen enlightenment in the interim. On the rare occasions there are lyrics, they will be by Samuel Beckett or some Gregorian monk. The packaging will consist of rough dung-coloured cardboard on which there is a very small photo of a sombre old man. He is looking into the distance rather than at us. There are no sleeve-notes, no dedications or grateful thanks, not even a kiss-my-arse from the producers. They must get through an awful lot of mineral water recording that stuff. Still mineral water, of course. Wouldn't want those bubbles to set off any inappropriate frivolity. But it's tranquil. Ooh, it's peaceful. Too peaceful for Sasha though.

'This is muesli music,' I tell him. 'I expected Wagner.'

'Personally, I find Wagner's use of German myth clumsy. In any case, I wanted you to hear the music I am going to overlay with the sounds of your death agonies. I find it amusing to sample the sound of fear. The pleading of the dying, the sounds of their agony. We call this "Darkwave". Ambient music for the strong.'

Is the use of 'overlay' correct? Is this the right time to quibble?

'You can't kill us,' says Sasha. 'I have original Brotherhood of Saturn papers. That's why we're really here. We were hoping to sell them.'

'You mean that junk we found in your bag? They are an amusing forgery. The Brotherhood of Saturn's papers were watermarked. And whoever wrote that nonsense had no understanding of Latin or Greek. It reads as if they have read something on the Internet and thought they could fake documents written by educated men. The arrogance is unbelievable.'

Sasha's protruding lower lip would definitely sway me, but the Dungeonmaster is made of sterner stuff, very stern stuff indeed, even sterner than her mad old dad.

'What happened to Jamie?' says Sasha.

'He's gone. He knows we have him on film killing someone. His silence is guaranteed. He was quite happy to go once he realised there was a misunderstanding about my work here. There are no experiments with animals.'

'You killed a cat!' says Sasha.

'Well, yes. But we don't *experiment* on animals. Not even humans. We just . . . release energy occasionally.'

And that's all we will be soon. Energy. Released from our rickety old skin-and-bone containers and left to roam free. Together for ever. Maybe *that's* the most frightening prospect.

'And he left us here!' says Sasha.

'I told him you had escaped. Otherwise he would have been most insistent on saving you. He is nothing if not chivalrous. I had the honour of being challenged to a duel by him. We eventually agreed that our strengths were different but roughly equal. He accepted a valuable knife from my collection, and honour was satisfied. Until he finds out that it is a fake, of course.'

The Dungeonmaster's laugh is fake too, and about as cheering as a yuletide sacrifice. 'The only thing that puzzles me is who you are working for. I have an extensive collection of torture instruments. Many have not been used for centuries for their rightful purpose. We will soon find out who sent you and why.'

'It was all my idea,' I tell him. 'You can let her go. She doesn't know anything about it.'

He stares at me for a while. But I actually mean it. Which I think surprises everyone present, not least myself.

'You surprise me,' he says. 'Perhaps there is hope for you yet.'

'It's the truth. I'll still be saying it whatever you do. Anyway, we came here to join you. I even got your symbol tattooed on my left arm.'

He follows my eye down my arm to where the Odin's Knot tattoo glistens. But it's still fresh and shiny, glinting on the top of my skin, yet to blend in underneath the surface.

'So what? Such a tattoo takes twenty minutes,' he says irrefutably. 'It can be covered up. After you have finished your assignment. V-men have used such tactics before.'

'What?'

He looks straight through me for a while. But I don't care because I honestly don't know what he is talking about.

'V-men. Undercover government agents.' He laughs harshly. 'You are either a brilliant actor or you are completely ignorant. But even if you are sincere, you are only a recent convert to our cause.'

'I was initiated into the Society of the Black Rose. I have carried their tattoo for twenty years.'

He examines this embarrassing remnant of my occult youth. It consists of a black sword with a black rose twined around it. It's not frightening unless you know anyone who was once part of the Society of the Black Rose. These dark luminaries mostly wanted to enjoy group sex and drugs in a genuinely sinister atmosphere – an entirely laudable aim – but they also attracted some seriously committed Nazis and unrepentant paedophiles. It's a familiar story: a perennial problem for disciples of My Lord Lucifer. And it is the sort of thing that gets Satanism a bad name. The Dungeonmaster nods as he examines the tattoo. He does know what it represents. I hope he doesn't know any of the principals involved, though, because I never joined. Or met any of them. It was just a cheap thrill, a cry for attention from the dark gods. But I'm glad I never got it covered up. Twenty years of apathy might finally be paying off. Until the Dungeonmaster shrugs his shoulders.

'So what?' he asks.

But he's right, of course. It is only a picture of a sword with a flower blooming from the left-hand side. This might signify evil, except that if you are standing opposite me the rose would be blooming from the right side, therefore signifying evil's exact opposite – Julie Andrews running up a hillside to launch into the opening salvo of *The Sound of Music* or Cliff Richard's triumphant victory over the demands of his own sperm.

'Look, we could have stayed in London. Having fun,' I say. Ain't *that* the truth? 'But we came here to serve.'

'Real commitment is more than scratching some symbol into your arm,' he says.

'Oh, no!' says Sasha. 'I need to clean up. I'm menstruating. I'm leaking all over your lovely clean stone . . .'

Many men would be less than overjoyed at this news. The Dungeonmaster is different. He cries out in triumph. 'It is a sign!' he says, addressing the rotating swastikas. 'The vision has come true!'

His eyes glow as he paces around the room, looking to enthuse the hooded figures in the shadows.

'A menstruating woman! Sent to guide us! Now I see it!'

The Dungeonmaster bows his head before Sasha.

'The sacred blood,' he says in an awe-struck whisper. 'The source of all life. The wise blood. Its wisdom is bestowed on all who channel the powers of the moon.'

I could mention the Spice Girls here. Or Bridget Jones. Or soap operas. Or *Hello!* magazine. That stuff doesn't seem all that *wise* to me. Sasha has already pointed out that what many men like is also no cause for celebration: football, motors, fighting and beer. And she may be right. She's certainly got the Dungeonmaster in a right old tizzy.

'Release them,' he says. 'They have earned the right to join us.'

As his hooded minions scurry to do his bidding, I experience a rare rush of pure joy. This is often the only reason to undergo these initiation ordeals – the magical equivalent of banging your head against a brick wall. Because it feels so good when it stops.

Once we are dressed the euphoria is really starting to build, especially after a glass of mulled wine. Until I focus on what the Dungeonmaster is actually saying to us. And it isn't about what time we are going to open our Xmas boxes.

'. . . if you really want to join us you must kill for the cause. Nothing less must do.' A left-handed smile slowly spreads over his otherwise impassive face. His eyes remain as bleak as a Newcastle Sunday. 'Are you committed?' he asks. 'Or are you a tourist?'

Suddenly he's beaming. Pure malevolence. *Schadenfreude* on stilts.

He disappears for a short while, then returns, wheeling a struggling, hooded figure tied to an operating table.

'This journalist wishes to expose our activities. I think she might well be an Israeli spy. She is certainly a Jew. Reason enough to kill her.'

He rips off her hood and reveals Kate's flushed and frightened face.

Kate is gagged by a thick black leather bit, on which the astrological sign for Saturn is emblazoned. Some might see this merely as a cross with a semicircle hanging off the lower right side. Anyone who has studied astrology might think it signified restriction, male authority, the harsh lessons that life can teach. And occult obsessives might think of the history of Teutonic black magic and the Brotherhood of Saturn. The only thing that really matters is that pleading look in Kate's eyes. Let me out. I didn't know it would be like this. Help me.

But there's nothing I can do. Except feel guilty about telling her about this place. Although that doesn't even help me, never mind the terrified woman in fear of her life.

'We found her snooping through my office,' says the Dungeonmaster. 'Interestingly enough, she is convinced that you are on my side. Which is keeping you alive presently. And we have a choice of sacrifice, a most uncommon luxury. If you wish to prove you are sincere about joining us, you will no doubt be willing to rid us of this genetic garbage.'

His mirthless smile chills me. For while I know I can't kill

Kate I couldn't be so sure about Sasha. In her present state. Her eyes are glassy, and that big purple bruise is spreading over her face. Just wait until she sees *that*; the Dungeonmaster won't stand a chance. Kate struggles as Sasha walks over to accept the knife. She pauses opposite him, taking a moment to get used to the feel of the weapon. Then she stares into his eyes. Surely she isn't going to plunge it into the Dungeonmaster? They would carve her to pieces afterwards. And although my life may have been a suicide mission, I thought Sasha was made of sterner stuff. But instead she walks right over to Kate, whose eyes are bulging out of their sockets. Sasha grabs the hair on the back of her head and pulls it to expose more of her throat. She places the cutting edge of the knife on Kate's neck. Breathing deeply, Sasha pauses to savour the moment, a smile that surely can't belong to her twisting her face.

'Stop!' says the Dungeonmaster. 'You have proved yourself worthy. It remains only to test your slave.' But he doesn't mean Stefan. He means me.

'Why test him again?' says Sasha. 'He was willing to sacrifice himself for me. Surely this is enough to prove his worth?'

It probably is the criterion by which Sasha judges men. But the Dungeonmaster may think differently.

'He may be devoted to you. But is he devoted to the Aryan race? Is he willing to fight for it? Will he even have the guts to fight for himself?'

The Dungeonmaster presents me with a sword.

'Take it. On the other side of that door, destiny awaits.'

As I take the weapon I can see love shining in Sasha's eyes. There is also insanity, a heady undercurrent of fermented moon-juice. I used to find that witch's brew very much to my taste. Being mad myself. But do I need it any more? Well, her skewed smile would seem to indicate that she has not had enough of me. She wants her hero to conquer whatever is on the other side of that door. It's time to say something memorable, as last words are supposed to last. But before I can think of anything the Dungeonmaster leads me up some steps to an imposing doorway. Sasha blows me a kiss. But the room beyond remains pitch-black, as dark and impenetrable as death itself.

'Fight well. And you will be rewarded,' says the Dungeonmaster.

The door shuts behind me. A heavy bolt secures it as light floods into my eyes. I am in an enclosed space the size of a squash court. There is blood up the walls. The floor is sticky. The air is foul. And soon I will be fighting for my life, again, just so that an overgrown child can be diverted from her real problem – herself. In the far corner of the chamber a thickset blond man is advancing with grim satisfaction. He has a broadsword and shield and has dressed for a twelfth-century massacre anywhere the Vikings came calling: horned helmet, blue cloak, leather jerkin and boots. He knows he will win. He has known he was going to win ever since his ancestors raped and pillaged their way across Europe. A smile starts to grow across his fat unshaven face as he advances. He reeks of beer, but he would have to be practically comatose to lose against me. He thrusts his sword towards me. I put everything I have into a savage sideswipe that is intended to send his weapon clattering into the corner. The sword stays fast.

By the time I have blocked a few more clumsy thrusts it might even look like this could be a contest. But he is just warming up.

His lumbering bulk comes after me with surprising speed

and agility, and there is nothing behind me except some unforgiving stone. The clash of metal mingles with the sweat of fear. A mad glint in his eyes seems to signal that he has finished his starter. It's time to carve into the main course.

He indulges himself in a belly laugh to emphasise his approaching triumph. His shoulders shake. His chins wobble. As he lurches towards me, he is so intent on sneering at me that he doesn't notice a puddle of blood left by the previous occupants. His leather sandals glide through the sticky puddle. He teeters on his slithery heels, then takes an experimental backward lunge that doesn't quite translate into flight. He lands badly, weighed down by his sword and shield. There is an ominous snick of bone and a strangled yelp of pain. I put the point of my sword in his side, at which he stays very still indeed, apart from the inevitable heaving of his great bloated belly. The slightest pressure of the sword would open up his stomach. But I can't do it. And it is exactly at this moment when a bell rings and the door is thrown open.

'Splendid!' says the Dungeonmaster, clapping me on the back. 'You are a man of honour! I would never have thought so! But I am delighted to have been wrong. Come, my dear fellow. We must celebrate. Your test is over.' He addresses a short burst of humiliating abuse at the man on the floor, who sits avoiding the Dungeonmaster's eyes. Sasha scampers in and kisses me, breath sour with wine and hunger.

'What about Kate?' I ask.

'That is no concern of yours,' says the Dungeonmaster. 'She will be detained for a while and then released. No one will believe this story of hers about creating a new life form. After all, who would be stupid enough to believe what they read on the Internet?'

Sasha stares back defiantly at me as the Dungeonmaster

starts to laugh. He carries on laughing until he sounds quite demented. I suppose it *is* easier to see the joke in other people's marriages. It's not quite so amusing for Sasha and me. Not funny at all. And the more he amuses himself at our expense, the more I could do with a beer.

'I need a drink,' I tell her.

'You need to stop!' she says.

And she's right. But just for today I'm going to get blind drunk. I mean, it *is* Xmas.

'Promise me!' she says.

'Of course! I'd rather be sober now anyway.'

'Or feeding your new cross-addiction to Ecstasy, grass, group sex . . . '

'Well, never mind about all that. I'll stop drinking in London.'

'I mean it.'

'So do I.'

Sasha turns to the Dungeonmaster. 'Can I call my mom? She's very ill. She might die at any time.'

The Dungeonmaster's face softens. 'Yes, of course. You can use my phone. Come, Matt. I will show you my favourite bar.'

12

THE BEER AND back-slapping with my new pal doesn't last long before his mobile rings with an urgent message. Then I'm left to wait for Sasha. This is something I have done a great deal of over the years. Although not usually in Alpine hunting lodges while twenty old people have Xmas lunch. Rather than look at them, I am facing a wall mounted with a life-size full-colour Jesus Christ, a plaster effigy complete with crucifix and crown of thorns. I know just how he feels. You keep saying the safe word and no one's listening. I have a few drinks with the birthday boy, trying as best as I might to ignore the cackle from the table behind me.

Two hours after the appointed time of arrival I am starting to think she might not be coming. But that might be the best solution anyway. I have had enough. I can't always rely on little puddles of blood to save my life, sacred or otherwise. Telling her it's over isn't going to be easy, but I have rehearsed the speech I am going to give her many times. It was embarrassing the first time the barmaid spotted me talking to myself, but I soon got over that. This is very good beer indeed. There's no point in drinking it slowly. Not after what we have just been through. And the more beer I have, the more certain I am that we should split up. Although I should maybe stick around and help her get better. But there isn't a cure for whatever it is she's got. And if there were, it wouldn't be me who found it. We're both mad, beyond help. Beyond even Prozac.

Another hour later, when the figure on the cross has started replying to my somewhat incoherent abuse, the waitress hands me an envelope with 'Matt' written on it. Inside are a thousand pounds, five thousand Deutschmarks and a faded beermat with 'I love you' written on it. I start to read her obsessively neat, neurotic handwriting: small and spiky, just like Sasha herself.

You probably don't remember writing 'I love you' on this beermat. You probably don't remember when you stopped saying it. Some time in the summer. I'll never forget you were prepared to sacrifice yourself to save me. But you don't love me any more. I'm going to see my mom. There might still be time. Don't follow me. Love Sasha xxx

I read it over and over again. But it's never going to say anything different. And once the reality of it hits me, it seems unlikely I will ever get off this stool. There is nowhere else to go. Nothing I want to do. Nothing left except a long, lingering, living death. The words in front of me start to blur. I can feel myself about to start a weeping fit that may end in me howling at the moon.

'So you *do* love me. Or is that self-pity?'

Sasha. Standing just close enough for a really good slap.

One open-handed swipe could knock that smile off her

face. And then a backhand return could remind her that I have had enough games for the moment.

'What if I had walked out that door?' I ask.

'I would have met you outside. You needed teaching a lesson. You've been taking me for granted.'

The cry of the neglected wife. But then we are married about five times over. It comes with the territory.

'I want to be back in London,' I tell her.

'I booked two flights from Munich.'

Sasha smiles. Even I couldn't argue with that. Although in my mind we are still going to get caught. What if someone finds Jake's body? What if Kate, in London, left some record of where she was going?

'You worry too much,' says Sasha, when I have put all this to her. For the moment it's me who looks raving mad while she just sits there, cool and calm against the backdrop of the snow-topped Alps.

'Somewhere up there is Hitler's mountain retreat,' says Sasha, much as she used to tell me where film stars lived in New York. We seem to have moved on to another sort of celebrity.

'These frustrated artists do sometimes exact a terrible revenge on the world,' I tell her. I wait to see if she will notice the similarity between her own life path and that of another badly parented short person. But instead she pats my hand.

'Don't feel bad about yourself,' she says, using her special soothing voice.

'I meant you,' I tell her. 'You and Hitler. You both like messing about with the occult. Even if you don't know what you're doing . . . '

'Don't I?'

'And you both like bossing other people about.'

She just sips her mineral water. She can hardly refute *that*. She taps her password into her hand-held computer.

'You've got all your evidence on that thing, right?'

She's avoiding my eyes. Perhaps ashamed of failure. She's let her daddy down. Again.

'Kate will make a programme about it,' I tell her. 'If they ever let her out.'

She smiles weakly. Avoiding my eyes. Perhaps some parental approval will help.

'You did it,' I tell her. 'You took 'em all on and won. I'm proud of you, babe.'

'Do you think so?' she says, her eyes pleading for more.

'You were right. I was wrong. You can still tell the world about the Dungeonmaster. You could tell those guys in London. The *Beacon*. They'll print it. I'm proud of you, babe.'

Daddy probably should have said those words to her once upon a time. Maybe he did and it just didn't take. But it's too late for anyone to say them now. Whatever she achieves, it will never be enough.

'We should get to the airport,' I tell her. 'We could still be arrested. Someone might find Jake's body. Or Werner's.'

'Or Kate's.'

'What?'

She can't help smiling. 'I killed your girlfriend. Kate.'

'What?'

'Don't look like that,' she says. 'We had to survive. Besides . . . no one else is having you. You're mine.'

I wait for a while for her to tell me this is a joke. But there is no apologetic smile. No shrug. No wink.

'When I went back for our stuff they had Kate staked out in a grove. Like where they used to strangle the sacrifices to Odin. It wasn't cruel. I slit her throat.'

She's played these games with me before. But this sounds real.

'She would have turned us in. She wanted that reward. For the Rob Powers thing. And she actually thought *we* were Nazis. The stupid bitch.'

I wait for the punchline. The smile which will say 'Fooled you! God, you're easy!' But it doesn't come. The punchline is that she has gone mad. For real, this time. And maybe irreversibly.

'And she wanted to take you away from me.'

'You're crazy. She hated me. And anyway, we have an open marriage,' I say, more of a question than a statement of fact.

'Not *that* open. She wasn't having you. Look, there was no paying her off. *They* offered her money, but she wasn't having it. She wasn't going to stop until she had exposed the Dungeonmaster or us or . . . and she would have taken you away from me.'

'That was the last thing she wanted.'

'It probably was. Now she's dead.'

She stops laughing when she sees my face. 'You're losing your sense of humour,' she tells me.

'It's not funny. Is this the fucking Prozac? Coming off it? After you doubled the dose?'

'You're the drug addict. You and your Ecstasy. At your age. I see clearly. I don't need antidepressants. My whole life has been pointing towards this. Where we are now.'

She takes a moment to congratulate herself. She is indeed thinking very clearly. Ice-cold logic. The triumph of the will.

'There really is no pleasing you. Is there? *She's dead! We're alive!*'

'I hear you.'

'Good. Now kiss me.'

It would have taken a braver man than me to refuse. When that's over, and I have failed to warm her cold lips, I ask her about Kate again. 'You wouldn't kill her. Just to join some stupid society.'

'Not to *join* it, no. But *running* it might be different.'

Her eyes are greyer than they used to be. More like the iron sky of Germany in winter. And a run of late nights and mortal terror have left spidery tracks of blood shot right through the whites of her eyes. I used to have difficulty in telling whether her eyes were blue, green, turquoise or whatever. Now I'm wondering who or what is in there.

'So you're the new head of the Black Order,' I say. 'You're not even German. You're certainly not a Nazi . . .'

Her most impish smile appears. 'Of course not. But my dad was. And he grew up just north of Munich. Like Stefan and Reinhard. That helped. Stefan voted for me.'

She smiles fondly. Lovely *loyal* Stefan. My little pony.

'Reinhard wants to go legit,' she says, 'to split from the Nazi idiots and get some real power. Centre politics with a slight nationalist flavour. It's what's working. All over the world. Jamie killing Werner really came in handy. It's the last link with the street-fighters. I'm going to be his press officer. I'm going to be really good at it.'

Public relations. Now that really *is* evil.

'My period starting like that was amazing . . . the sacred blood. Reinhard thought it was high time a woman took control. That was the sign.'

'I think I preferred it when you called him the Dungeon-master.'

'And killing Kate was the clincher. It meant I was the real thing.' She pats my hand reassuringly. Her icy touch does nothing to warm my frozen blood.

'You worry too much,' she continues. 'We don't have to get mixed up with the politics if you don't want to. That's just show business anyway. We can just play with Reinhard's money. And travel. And do whatever we like.'

'It's not funny,' I tell her, but she's staring out at the Alps. My little ice-maiden. Home at last.

She's wearing the Saturn symbol around her neck, a dark red stain on a shining black stone. For some it represents paternal authority. Maybe she has found a way of defeating her father. She has certainly surpassed him. For he never got as far as taking command.

The Greeks' version of the Roman Saturn was Kronos, the creator of time. I suppose time will tell if this isn't just an elaborate fiction to liven up what might appear to be a slow morning after our recent excitements. But I can't wait. I have to know.

'You wouldn't. You couldn't,' I tell her. Although it's looking increasingly like I'm telling myself what I want to hear. Her eyes are cold, grey bullets with traces of dried blood.

'You'll never really know,' she says. 'Will you?'

Also by Mark Ramsden and published by Serpent's Tail

The Dark Magus and the Sacred Whore

'Lashings of black magic, kinky sex, and bad jokes in this agreeably distasteful little book' *Sunday Times*

'A dryly witty murder mystery... the writing quality is superior, the style fast-paced and darkly comic... this is definitely one for those who believe SM fiction shouldn't be reduced to the level of Mills & Boons with bondage' *Skin Two*

'A baroque, uproarious parody of every genre you could think of... you'll laugh along until your piercings ache' *Time Out*

'A neo-noir tale of perversion and madness, and a wildly offbeat love story. Well worth a look!' *Preview*

'A weirdly entertaining romp involving bodies in freezers, foot fetish videos, the roadie from hell... It's exactly the sort of book for which maverick publishing houses like Serpent's Tail were designed' *Forum*

'Cheese graters, rubber, ageing rock stars, black magic internet sites, dead drug dealers, missing penises, dodgy Sarf London geezers, cocaine and cyberincest in New York. Perverted, witty and absolutely hilarious debut from the editor of *Fetish Times*' *Stuff*

'The deliciously dark debut novel from *Fetish Times* editor and occasionally *Desire* contributor Mark Ramsden. A neo-noir tale of perversion and madness involving dominatrixes, pimps and sacred whores' *Desire*

Meet Matt. He's an Englishman in New York. He's in New York because he has a very bad temper, so bad the other guy died of it. But he's doing all right in NYC, running a satanic services scam over the internet.

Meet Sasha. She's Matt's live-in deity, a New Age sex magician. To pay the bills she has a little sideline, torturing a rock 'n' roll star in her private dungeon.

Meet Nails. He's a heavy duty drug dealer from the 'hood. Oh, and he's also the dead guy on Matt and Sasha's floor.

A high-octane ultra-noir thriller and a savagely funny New Age satire, *The Dark Magus and the Sacred Whore* is crime fiction from way out on the cutting, tattooing and piercing edge.

The Dungeonmaster's Apprentice

'Fine black-hearted fun' *Time Out*

'Despite the stream of wisecracks, *The Dungeonmaster's Apprentice* has disturbing undercurrents that will make it linger in your memory like a prolonged whipping. A worthy follow-up to a truly skewed original' *Forum*

'A wonderfully bloody and uproarious romp set amongst the disparate strands of alternative lifestylers that make up London's fetish scene . . . A sardonic wit sharp enough to cut cocaine with, Ramsden sets about savagely lampooning the pompous pretensions of those transgressive aspirants who lurk in the darker shadows of the SM underground' *Desire*

'A revealing and surprisingly accessible thriller . . . Ramsden's dry wit ensures the journey is as funny as it is compelling. Oh, and it's very rude' *Minx*

'Lashings of humour, generally of a hue blacker than a thigh-high leather boot' *Big Issue*

'This titillating original novel hails from the dark depths of Ramsden's twisted imagination . . . Weird, but great' *Front*

Matt and his partner the Supreme Ogress Sasha, a 5'2" dominatrix have fled New York leaving a trail of bodies behind them. Back in London ripping off the fetish scene, their daily routine is abruptly shattered by a sinister death threat from the Dungeonmaster's Apprentice. To make matters worse, the threat comes delivered in a highly undesirable package containing the skull of a dead cat, Matt and Sasha's names written backwards in what can only be blood, and a picture of them torn to shreds.

An unfortunate fatality at a fetish event and Sasha's desire to infiltrate a neo-Nazi sect do not set them back on the road to safety and they are sucked into the unpredictable realm of the occult . . .

A dark and devilishly funny follow-up to Mark Ramsden's debut, the highly acclaimed *The Dark Magus and the Sacred Whore*.